Strands of Fate

Library of Congress-in-Publication Data
Strands of Fate / by Linda Kozar
p. cm.
I. Title
2012913007

CreativeWomanMysteries.com
800-282-6643
Creative Woman Mysteries
Series Editor: Shari Lohner

10 11 12 13 14 | Printed in China | 10 9 8 7 6 5 4 3

Fate is not an eagle, it creeps like a rat.
~ Elizabeth Bowen

Wainscott, Scotland

— Prologue —

"Have you located the McClain woman?" demanded the voice on the phone.

"I have." The man known as "Snake" adjusted his cap to better hide his face. He owed his nickname to the large cobra tattooed along the side of his neck.

"You're clear about what I need for you to do?"

"Aye." He licked his lips, his gaze fixed on the garden cottage down the lane. Through his windshield, he watched a striking, red-haired woman emerge from a small building next to her cottage.

"You understand failure is not an option?"

"I understand," he said.

"I was told you're one of the best. Don't make me regret hiring you."

Snake squeezed his cellphone so tightly that the plastic crackled in his grip. He didn't like being bossed around. But the dismal state of his bank account demanded he swallow his pride for the moment. "I can handle the woman."

"See that you do," the voice replied, and the line went dead.

— 1 —

A sharp rap at the door startled Shannon McClain in mid-stitch, causing her to prick her index finger with her embroidery needle. She winced and brought the finger to her mouth.

"One moment, please."

She rose from her chair and made her way to the front door. When she opened it, she found the stoop empty. Perplexed, she glanced to the right and to the left but saw only rows and rows of flowerpots overflowing with blooms. *How odd.*

She closed the door and went back to her handwork, a delicate pillowcase edging. She hoped her quick reaction had kept blood from soiling the cloth. Though close to finishing this particular project, she'd decided to add an extra row of seed pearls to the hummingbird's wing to highlight the tip.

Shannon had gained a name for herself, beading necklaces with precious and semiprecious stones, Italian glass, and antique findings. Recently she'd begun incorporating her beading designs into embroidered handwork, along with knitted caps and sweaters. And she was finding it hard to keep up with the new orders.

Perhaps, as her best friend, Coleen, said, she was too much of a perfectionist. But Shannon never regretted going the extra mile for a client. The client who'd ordered the pillowcases for a wedding gift was sure to be content.

Rap-rap-rap. Aggravation rising, she put down her work and opened the door again.

"Aaaargh!" A woman jumped out from behind a bush next to the porch, her face hidden behind a fierce-looking tribal mask. She waved her arms wildly in the air.

"An ainm an àigh!" Shannon bent over to catch her breath as the woman removed her mask. "Oh, for heaven's sake, Coleen. You almost scared me to death."

"Isn't she a beauty?" Coleen held up the mask with pride. "She's a perfect fit for my collection."

"Lovely," Shannon replied, her voice flat.

"Say, you're a bit on edge today, aren't you?" Coleen sauntered through the open door, carrying the mask and a newspaper. "I'd fancy a cup of tea. If we're still on speaking terms, that is."

"We are—just barely." Shannon winked. "Follow me to the kitchen and I'll start the tea."

As Coleen took a seat at the table, Shannon set the tea kettle on the cooker and glanced at her friend. The two could not have been more different in appearance. Coleen's light brown hair hung stick straight to her shoulders, a sharp contrast to Shannon's wavy red locks. And Coleen stood a full head taller. Yet, despite their many differences, their hearts were well matched. Her friend had proven to be a faithful anchor through the years. The untimely death of Shannon's husband, John, three years earlier had taken her to the brink of despair. Were it not for Coleen's tender care and concern ...

With the newspaper spread open on the table before her, Coleen offered a running commentary of what she read.

"Will you look at this article? Dieticians say pork scratchings are good for you. Imagine that. One day they're bad for you, the next day they're fine. I'll never figure it out." Coleen made a pretense of sniffing the air. "Speaking of food, what is that heavenly scent? Not your fabulous lemon scones?"

Shannon smiled. "You know very well I bake them every week for Crafternoon."

Shannon treasured the once-a-week gathering of friends in her home, which had been nicknamed "Crafternoon" by none other than Coleen. The group had developed close ties over the years. Each week, the ladies worked on a different craft together, sometimes for gifts or for their own homes. Other times, they worked on special projects to give to elderly shut-ins, orphanages, or for overseas missions.

Coleen frowned. "Oh, about today's Crafternoon ..."

"What?"

"The others can't make it. Ginny had to take her mother to a doctor's appointment."

"What about Rebecca and Pauline?" Shannon asked.

"Rebecca tried coloring her own hair and made a mess of it. She's having a technician do a fix today."

"What color is it?"

"Pink."

"Oh my. And Pauline?"

Her friend licked her finger to help turn to the next page. "Her cat's sick again. She's taking it to the vet."

"I think she spends more time and money on that cat than her own children."

"I agree. But between you and me, her cat's a lot nicer."

Shannon chuckled. As she moved to join Coleen at the table, she glanced into the living room. Through the front windows she noticed her neighbor's car pull into the drive across the lane.

"I'm really starting to worry about Mrs. Campbell living alone." Shannon watched through the glass as something that could only be described as a human-sized bug tried to free itself from the driver's seat of her neighbor's compact car. "I think her mind is slipping."

Coleen leaned back in her chair to peer around Shannon. "So she likes to dress up as the Book Bug when she volunteers at the children's library. What's wrong with that?"

"She volunteers at the library one day a week. I see her in that costume every day."

Mrs. Campbell finally managed to get both of her human legs and all of the fuzzy bug legs out of the car. But she continued to struggle against the puffy body of the costume still wedged between the seat and the steering wheel.

"Should we help her?" Coleen asked, trying not to laugh.

"No, I've learned that only makes her mad. Give her a second."

Within moments, the giant bug broke free from the seat and staggered a few steps across the lawn. Then it returned to the car to pull a grocery bag from the backseat.

Coleen gasped. "She goes to the market dressed like that?"

"And that's not even what worries me the most." Shannon turned away from the window and walked back to the counter. She plated a tray of fresh lemon scones pulled from the oven less than an hour before, and placed them on the table. "Since you fancy a cup of tea, how about a lemon scone to go with it?"

"Don't mind if I do." Coleen lifted a scone to her mouth. "So, back to Mrs. Campbell—you were saying?"

"Honestly, I think she suffers from paranoia. Every day this week, she's told me to watch out for the 'snake man.' She's convinced he's lurking around the neighborhood, spying on us."

"Did you say 'snake man'?"

"Mmm-hmm."

"What is *that* exactly?"

"I've no idea. She doesn't elaborate."

The kettle let out a shrill whistle. Shannon poured a small amount of the steaming water into her favorite teapot, a blue delft she'd received from her father before leaving for college. Though some people skipped this "warming" step, Shannon believed a true tea enthusiast would never pass on the opportunity to ensure that the tea brewed at the optimum temperature. After swirling the hot water around, she emptied the pot, added tea leaves, and filled the pot with more hot water.

"Has she called the police?" Coleen asked.

Shannon nodded. "Yes, but they don't take her seriously when she calls anymore. So she reports her 'sightings' to me now. She's warned me in person, by phone, and with notes tacked to my door. The whole situation is starting to make me feel a little nutty myself."

"Don't let it upset you. It's wonderful she has you so close to keep an eye on her."

"I suppose." Shannon turned away, but not before her friend caught the frown on her face.

"I don't like that look," Coleen said.

"I've been thinking, what if she's *me* in thirty years?"

"Don't be ridiculous." Coleen took another bite of her scone. "Why would you say such a thing?"

"In many ways, we're a lot alike." Shannon set two teacups on the counter. "We both live alone."

"Everyone who lives alone isn't nuts. Besides, you've only lived alone since Alec and Lara left for college last fall. Not nearly enough time to go crazy."

"Her husband died when she was young." Shannon sighed, her thoughts turning to John. "As did mine."

"Being a young widow doesn't mean you're destined to finish life in a bug costume. And you know I'd never let you out of your house in a getup like that."

"We both love plants," Shannon countered.

"You don't name yours."

"Not yet."

Coleen continued. "And you also don't bake them birthday cakes, complete with candles that come near to burning your lawn to a crisp."

They both burst out laughing.

"That was a day to remember, wasn't it?" Shannon asked as she strained the hot tea into cups. "I suppose you're right. There might be a sliver of hope for me. Thanks for the pep talk."

"What are friends for?"

An ear-piercing scream sounded through the open window in the front room. "Snake! Snake! It's the snake man!"

"Mrs. Campbell?" Shannon set the teapot down and hurried to the window. Coleen followed, close on her heels.

Through the glass, they saw Mrs. Campbell jumping up and down in front of a FedEx truck parked in the lane, her bare arms and fuzzy bug legs flailing. The driver lay on the ground in Shannon's yard, clinging to a package, while struggling to fend off blows from a larger man dressed entirely in black.

"Och!" Shannon grabbed a can of spray lacquer from a bead kit on the end table closest to her and raced out the door.

"What are you going to do, glaze him?" Coleen yelled after her. Then she snatched the fire poker off the hearth. "Wait for me!"

When the attacker saw his audience increase, he jumped off the driver and fled, but not before Shannon spotted the tattoo on his neck. *A snake.*

No longer in need of a weapon, Shannon dropped the spray can and hurried to help the driver, her long-time friend, to his feet. "Ethan, what happened? Are you all right?"

Ethan stood up, his legs a little unsteady. He tried to straighten his glasses, now slanted precariously on his nose, but one side of the frame was bent. "I'm fine. Lucky for that hooligan you came along. I was about to teach him a hard lesson he wouldn't soon forget."

"Aye." Shannon felt her lips twitch. "That was my concern. Why did he attack you?"

Ethan held out a package. "I can only assume the thief wanted to get his hands on your jewelry supplies. Perhaps he thinks this is filled with diamonds."

Shannon took the box, now dented on one corner, and studied the return address. "That's odd. I'm not expecting a bead shipment from the United States."

"Then what is it?" Coleen demanded.

"I have no idea."

"I *warned* you about the snake man, but you thought I was crazy. Who's crazy now, hmmm?"

Shannon, Ethan, and Coleen turned to find Mrs. Campbell glaring at them, her hands on the puffy costume at about the height her hips should be.

She didn't wait for a reply. "I'm calling the police. Maybe *this* time they'll listen." With that, she marched across the lane, squeezed through her front door and slammed it shut behind her.

"Be careful, Shannon," Ethan warned. "That man might return."

Shannon smiled fondly at him. "I don't think the thief will come back now that we've all seen him. No doubt he'll find another neighborhood to haunt. Thank you for making sure he didn't get my package."

"All in a day's work." Ethan winked at the women and limped back to his truck.

The moment she stepped inside, Shannon opened the box, careful to preserve the return address. She'd never heard of "Barnwell, Meecham & Hanscombe," but it seemed they knew her.

Inside the box she found two items—a letter sealed in a thick gray envelope, and a small bag made of silk. She ripped open the letter and sank into a nearby chair. She felt her hands begin to tremble as she read.

"What's wrong?" Coleen asked.

"It's from a U.S. law firm."

Coleen leaned forward. "What do they want?"

Shannon took a deep breath and handed the letter to Coleen. "Read it aloud. Maybe I'll believe it from your lips."

Eyes wide, Coleen took the letter and began to read.

Dear Mrs. McClain,

As the executors of the last will and testament of our client, Victoria Elizabeth Paisley, it is incumbent upon us to inform you of her recent demise. Please accept our sincere condolences.

Your grandmother willed to you, her granddaughter, a sizable portion of her estate. She has appointed you as the sole owner of her residence and fifteen acres of surrounding property on 2121 Larkspur Lane, in the town of Apple Grove, Oregon, as well as her business, The Paisley Craft Market & Artist Lofts, located at 7 South Main Street, also in the town of Apple Grove, Oregon. Both are to be run or disposed of as you see fit.

However, Mrs. McClain, there are legal and financial issues which cannot be delayed. It is imperative, if you choose to claim this inheritance, that you arrive at our offices in Apple Grove for the reading of the will on April 18 at 10:30 a.m. Pacific Standard Time.

If you fail to appear for the reading of the will, please be advised that in accordance with your grandmother's wishes, we will be forced by the terms of the will to regard your inheritance as null and void, and the balance of the estate will be sold at a public auction and subsequently divided among the remaining heirs. Please notify us of your decision as soon as possible.

Enclosed you will find an heirloom locket, Mrs. Paisley dictated that it be given to you upon her passing.

Sincerely,
Roger T. Barnwell
Attorney at Law
Barnwell, Meecham & Hanscombe

Shannon shook her head in disbelief. "April 18? But that's only eight days from now. This must be some kind of mistake. Or a joke. I don't know anyone named Victoria Paisley."

"But you don't know much about your mother or her family, do you?" Coleen asked, a gentle lilt to her voice. "Isn't it possible this woman could've been your maternal grandmother?"

"It's possible, I suppose." Shannon dared to believe it for a moment. Could this letter be the clue she'd waited for all her life?

At the tender age of four, Shannon had suffered a devastating blow when her mother vanished without a trace. Her mother, Beth, left the house one morning to take a letter to the post office, and she never returned. Shannon knew very little about her or the circumstances surrounding her disappearance—only what her father would tell her, and that wasn't much. It was clear, even to her four-year-old self, that her mother's disappearance had left a scar on her father's heart he would carry until the day he died.

As would Shannon.

Coleen's voice interrupted her memories. "If Victoria truly was your grandmother, according to this letter, you're to be rich. Oh my goodness!" Coleen clasped her hands together. "That would solve your money problems. I know the insurance money from John's death is almost gone."

"I can't believe this is happening. It seems so surreal." Shannon paused, remembering how she'd felt earlier that morning, as though *something* was waiting for her. Could this be it? Could this be the next step in her life? "The letter said 'craft market,' right? An *arts and crafts* market?"

"Yes!" Coleen exclaimed. "And I can think of nothing more perfect for you."

"But, wait a minute … if there are other heirs, why would she leave everything to me?"

"I don't know. I suppose you'll find out on April 18." Coleen pointed to the blue silk bag. "Please open it now. I can't stand the suspense."

Shannon reached for the small bag and loosened the silken string gathering the closure. The gleam of a silver chain caught her eye. She wrapped her index finger around it and lifted it to the light. At the end of the chain dangled a delicate locket inlaid with amethysts, pearls, and emeralds.

Coleen gasped. "I've never seen anything so lovely."

Shannon studied the locket with anticipation, knowing such pieces often contained family keepsakes. Then she turned it over, hoping to learn where the piece originated. "Look, it's from Tiffany's in New York."

"Tiffany's?" Coleen wrinkled her nose.

Shannon cradled the locket in her palm for a closer look, and then she slid a fingernail along the crease in the side. It took almost no pressure to open the piece. Inside, from a faded picture, a young girl dressed in her Sunday best, a beautiful dress with smocking on the collar, stared back at her. Though in black and white, the resemblance was irrefutable.

Shannon trembled, tears springing to her eyes. "It's her."

"Who?"

"My mother."

Her friend reached for the locket. "May I?"

Shannon placed the locket in Coleen's hand.

"Why, it's uncanny. Even though she's only a child in this picture, it's easy to see you're related. Your grandmother must have worn this locket close to her heart all the days of her life."

Shannon did not respond, but she continued to stare at the locket.

Coleen shook her head. "She must have suffered so, losing her daughter, not knowing if she still walked the earth. Can you imagine?"

"I can," Shannon whispered.

Coleen drew a hand to her mouth. "Oh, my goodness, I'm so sorry." She wrapped her hand around Shannon's. "I'm always bumpin' my gums. Of course you know what it's like. She disappeared from your life too. It seems you and your grandmother had something in common."

"Unless Victoria knew what became of my mother. What if she kept in contact with her or another member of her family after she left us? Supposing she was still alive, that is."

At a loss for words, Coleen bit her lip.

"I'd like to wear it," Shannon said.

"I'll help you put it on." Coleen stood and positioned herself behind her friend.

She placed the locket around Shannon's neck and closed the clasp in the back. "Let's have a look in the mirror."

The two women walked to a gilded mirror near the front door. Sunlight streamed in through windows on either side. Shannon's long red hair, vibrant as autumn, came to life, standing out in breathtaking contrast against the forest green of her sweater. Her blue eyes, translucent as jewels, reflected facets of emotions back at her—worry, surprise, and fear.

The locket was even more astounding in the sunlight. The amethysts and emeralds sparkled. Its pearls gleamed with an aged patina. The beauty of the piece took her breath away.

Coleen's reflection appeared behind her friend's. She rested her chin on Shannon's shoulder. "It's gorgeous, especially on you."

"Thank you." Shannon took a deep breath. "This locket has convinced me, the package was not sent here by mistake. Victoria was my grandmother."

"So you'll travel to America for the reading of the will?"

"Yes. I hope while I'm there I can learn more about my mother. I'll leave for Oregon as soon as possible."

"Then I'm going with you."

"You'd come with me?"

"Of course I would. You're not setting foot on American soil without your best friend by your side."

Shannon tilted her head, resting it against her friend's. "If you put it that way, then I suppose I have no choice but to take you along. How will your dear husband survive all alone?"

"Now that you mention it, I don't know. The man can't find his socks without me. I'll arrange for the girls to look in on him while I'm gone. How long do you think we'll be there? A week or two at least, wouldn't you say? What should we wear? Perhaps I'll take my new cashmere wrap."

Shannon grinned. "So now you're asking and answering your own questions, I see. No need to converse with anyone; you do a fine job of conversing with yourself."

Her friend laughed. "You've got me pegged, don't you? Oh, Shannon, you're such a dear friend. I'm going to miss you. Now that you've come into wealth, I hope you don't forget about your lowly friend who lives in a cottage by the sea."

Shannon stepped away and turned to face her friend. "You talk as if I've moved away. I have no intention of moving to America. Scotland is my home."

"Hmmph." Coleen turned away and walked back to the kitchen to reclaim her plate. She broke off a piece of scone, and popped it into her mouth. "If it turns out you're as rich as Rockefeller, you won't be interested in sticking around *this* little village. You'll be living the high life somewhere much more exciting."

Shannon folded her arms across her chest. "That'll be the day. My *life* is here. I'll travel to Apple Grove, but only long enough to meet what remains of my mother's family and put the property and the business up for sale. The proceeds should provide enough for me and my children to live off of. I'll invest some of it into the online business too. If you ask me, this is a pure blessing from above, but not one to change my whole life."

"Time will tell, my friend." Coleen regarded her fondly. "But I wouldn't be so sure about all of that. One never knows what fate has in store."

— 2 —

Shannon went to work right away and reserved their train tickets, booked their flights, and made rental car arrangements for the trip. She also signed up for an international phone plan in anticipation of the calls she would make to the twins.

When she called the law firm in Oregon to confirm her intention to attend the reading of the will, the attorney offered to have his assistant reserve a room for her at a nearby inn.

Less than a week later, as she packed her last suitcase for the trip, the sound of a thump against the back of the cottage and retreating footsteps stopped her cold.

She grabbed the phone off her nightstand and crept down the hall toward a window at the rear of the house. Just as she got close enough to look out, a bird appeared and fluttered its wings against the glass.

"Och!" Shannon dropped the phone, her heart racing. She listened intently. No sound could be heard outside. As if in slow motion, she moved to the door, unlocked it, and twisted the knob.

She opened it a few inches and peered through the crack. There was no one outside. She opened it wider still and saw an envelope nailed to the doorway trim. It was plain white with "Shannon" scrawled across the front in dripping rivulets of red.

She tore it off the nail and slammed the door shut.

With trembling fingers, she opened the envelope, slid out the single sheet of plain white paper, and unfolded it.

At the top of the sheet was printed: *"STAY AWAY FROM APPLE GROVE … OR ELSE."*

Trying not to panic, she strode to the kitchen, and tossed the messy envelope in the trash. Then she poured herself a cup of tea, and collapsed into a chair at the table. After a few sips, she took a deep breath and reread the note. By the fifth read she felt certain there was no real reason to be alarmed.

This must be the work of Mrs. Campbell.

After the "snake man" incident, her neighbor's strange behavior had increased twofold. She continued to leave notes on Shannon's door about suspicious activities she observed in the neighborhood—everything from a new car parked on the lane to a helicopter flying too low overhead.

A new wave of unease crept over Shannon as she continued to sip her tea and contemplate the note. The handwriting looked nothing like Mrs. Campbell's usual scrawl. And she'd certainly never written anything using a substance that resembled blood.

When Shannon heard the unmistakable sound of a key turning the lock in the front door, she almost dumped her tea in her lap. The door swung open and familiar voices called out for her.

"What's this?" She shoved the note into her pocket and jumped up, surprised to see her son, Alec, and daughter, Lara, stroll in. "What are you two doing here?"

Her unease about the note melted away as she pulled them into her arms. "I repeat, what are you doing here?

You're supposed to be in school. And you don't have a vehicle. How did you get here?"

"We bummed a ride from our mate," Alec answered.

"Who?"

"Kenneth."

"Is he going to take you back? You know I can't. I'm leaving for Oregon in the morning."

Lara kissed her on the cheek. "We know. That's why we're here, to send you off proper. Kenneth is leaving this evening, and he's agreed to take us back with him."

Alec stroked his chin in mock concern. "Aren't you glad to see us? Should we go?" He turned as if to carry out his bluff.

She grabbed him by the collar and held him tight. "Am I glad? Does the smile on my face say anything about the way I feel?"

She regarded her teenage children, fraternal twins, with adoration. Alec's wavy red hair had lightened a bit, probably from all the time he spent fishing when he was supposed to have his nose in a book. A few locks hung a bit too close to his eyes, deep green and wise beyond their years. It seemed as if he'd grown taller too, but then again, both children had towered over her for years.

Though her father never spoke of it, from pictures, Shannon knew Lara was the spitting image of her own mother, Beth. She looked her daughter over. Skin like cream, sparkling green eyes, and, like Alec, she had the glow of health about her. Lara wore her long red hair piled in a loose bun atop her head with curls cascading down around her face and at the nape of her neck.

Alec dropped his backpack onto the floor. "What's for

dinner? I'm famished."

"Oh, so it's dinner you want, is it?" Shannon laughed. "Whatever your heart desires."

"Mine desires fish-and-chips." He produced an insulated sack from his bag. "Caught and cleaned this morning. And please make 'em crispy—"

"On the edges," she finished his sentence. "I know how you like your fish fried, son."

Shannon gave her daughter's arm a squeeze. "And for you, my dear? What will you have?"

"I'd like a potato-and-egg frittata."

"A what? Frittata?"

"I have a roommate from Spain. It's her favorite dish, and she taught me how to make it."

"Good, because I haven't a clue."

Lara laughed. "Don't worry, Mum. I'll be the one making it. You'll be the one eating."

"If you insist." She wrapped her arms around their shoulders, one on either side. "You don't know what it means to have you home. I appreciate the trouble you went to so you could be here."

"We couldn't let you leave the country without a proper goodbye," Alec answered. "Besides, you'll be gone for a couple of weeks, and if a young man like myself were to crave a home-cooked meal, I'd be out of luck, wouldn't I?"

"I suppose you would. We'd better get busy in the kitchen then. I'm so happy I could swoon."

They'd scarcely begun the food preparation when the front door swung open, blowing a blast of wind and leaves into the house.

"Anybody home? It's me." Coleen breezed into the room and threw her arms around Alec and Lara. "Sorry about the mess; the wind's picking up. I heard you two were here. Ran into Kenneth's mum at the market. The only thing that kept me from running straight here were the groceries I had to put away first."

She stood back to look them over. "Lara, you're a tad too thin. And you," Coleen squinted at Alec, "I can tell you're still full of mischief."

"Can you join us for dinner?" Shannon asked. "We're having quite the feast."

"I wish I could, but since I'm leaving my darling tomorrow to travel halfway around the world, I thought I should spend my last night at home with him. I'm going to cook him a special dinner." She winked. "A *romantic* dinner."

Alec made a gagging sound.

Coleen gave him a playful cuff on the shoulder. "Oh, so you think people stop living after they turn forty, do you? Well, we don't. You'll see one day."

"If you won't stay for dinner, at least have some tea while we rattle around the kitchen," Shannon invited.

"That I will do," Coleen answered. "Did you happen to make your scones? I'd never turn down one of those."

Shannon pursed her lips. "Sorry. Since we're leaving tomorrow, I didn't. I've been cleaning out the fridge, trying to finish off the perishables."

"I figured as much." Coleen waved at her. "Get busy cooking the family feast. I'll set the table for you while we all talk."

As Coleen passed Shannon, she nudged her arm and

whispered, "OK, I know that look. What's wrong?"

"What? Nothing." Still undecided as to whether or not to tell Coleen about the note, Shannon flashed a reassuring smile. "I'm a little anxious about the trip, that's all."

Coleen cocked one eyebrow. "Not having second thoughts about going, are you?"

"Absolutely not. Nothing could change my mind. I'm going to Apple Grove, and I plan to get some answers."

* * *

Later that night, the light of a full moon coaxed Shannon out of a fitful sleep. She rose and slipped on a robe for warmth against the chill of the night. Leaning on the wall next to her bedroom window, she gazed out at the night sky. A galaxy of stars winked back at her. But the moon, in full resplendence, dominated her attention. Its luminescence had a hypnotic effect on her.

She sighed.

Drawing her arms in close to hug her body, she considered going back to bed. But an odd feeling of restlessness stirred within her, so she began to wander.

The kitchen, washed in moonlight, brought back happy memories of family dinners around the table, the children laughing, full of vibrancy and happy mischief. She'd spent many a lonesome night since the twins left for their university studies. Quiet nights. Quiet days. Quiet everything in between.

She'd put on a brave face for Alec and Lara the day she moved them to their respective dorm rooms. No need for them to see her tearful and upset. Through no less than gargantuan efforts, her eyes remained dry and her smile intact during a short tour of the university. But during the hour-long ride back to Wainscott alone, she'd nearly fallen to pieces. Saying goodbye to them this evening had been no easier, but she relished the wonderful dinner they'd shared. The fish Alec brought home were delicious, and Lara's frittata was superb.

She made her way down a short hallway to the study. A large wooden desk occupied the lion's share of the room. Two of the walls were covered floor to ceiling with mahogany bookshelves loaded to capacity with books, souvenirs from holidays, and interesting rocks collected on hiking trips. Her husband, like her father, had enjoyed a thriving career as a geologist. When the two men would get together and go on about rocks, there was no stopping them.

She slipped into a wingback chair facing the desk. The sudden coolness of the leather against her thin robe sent a shiver through her body. How John had loved spending his time in the company of books. Seated in a matching oxblood chair, his feet propped up on the top of the desk, her husband would lean back and read for hours on end. In her mind's eye, she could still see him sitting there, brow slightly furrowed, as it did whenever he was deep in thought.

Here the moon intruded as well. Through a porthole window close to the ceiling, a shaft of beautiful translucent light illuminated the plane tickets she'd printed and laid out on top of the desk. Tomorrow afternoon, she and Coleen would be on their way to New York, and later they'd catch another plane bound for Portland.

She surveyed the room, picking up each and every detail available in the limited light. Try as she might, Shannon couldn't shake the feeling that she would never again live in her dear little home.

Her eyes soon settled on a knitting basket tucked near the end of a top shelf. She rose from her chair and pulled the basket down. In it, she found a scarf, perhaps a quarter of the way finished, wrapped around her two favorite knitting needles. Though not clearly visible in the darkness of the room, she knew exactly what the scarf looked like. It was a charming creation of brown, burgundy, and gray yarns. A manly combination of colors, and fittingly so, for the scarf was to have been for John. She'd sat in the very same chair, knitting it, the day he died. And later that same day, after she'd received the horrific news of her husband's fate, she'd shoved the basket to the top shelf and washed her hands of it.

She pressed the scarf against her cheek, a tender relic of the past. *John, how I wish you were here with me. You'd surely know what to make of all of this.*

A short while later, she wandered back to bed and slipped between the cool sheets. Although her body desired rest, her mind wouldn't allow it. There were too many unanswered questions running through her head.

Though she'd grown up in a loving home, the best her father could manage, she'd always felt incomplete without her mother. Somewhere in the world, if her mother lived, the woman who bore her breathed the same air and gazed at the same moon. Did she ever wonder about the daughter she'd left behind? What had she chosen over a life with her family? Perhaps answers would be waiting for her in Apple Grove.

Shannon closed her eyes and tried to sleep. Morning could not come soon enough.

— 3 —

"The attorney wouldn't tell you who else might be at the reading of Victoria's will?" Coleen had spent the better part of the half-hour train ride to Glasgow's International Airport barraging Shannon with questions. "That seems odd to me. Doesn't he understand how curious you are about your family?"

"He didn't say he *wouldn't* tell me. He just didn't."

"You mean you didn't ask?"

Shannon rubbed her temples, feeling a headache threaten to take hold. "I can't recall what my exact words were. Did you remember to bring a book to read during the flight?"

Coleen laughed. "Sorry. I can tell I'm making you nuts. Yes, I did bring a book. But I don't plan to read it; I plan to sleep. Remember?" She fished in her purse and pulled out a sandwich bag containing a handful of prescription sleeping pills, and dangled them in the air for Shannon to see.

"Oh, that's right. You're afraid of take-offs and landings."

"I am not *afraid* of them. I just find them unpleasant and choose not to consciously experience them. Much like someone who doesn't like onions avoids eating them. They don't avoid onions because they're frightened by them. They simply choose not to experience them."

Shannon suppressed a grin. Her fearless friend would

never admit to having a phobia. There was no point in trying to push the issue.

As the train rolled to a stop, Shannon was overcome with an uneasy feeling, like someone was watching her. It was the second time she'd felt it since they left Wainscott. She turned in her seat to look down the aisle behind her. No one paid her any attention.

I'm letting Mrs. Campbell's ridiculous note get to me.

"This is our stop." Coleen sprang up out of her seat. She gathered her bags and exited the train as Shannon struggled to catch up.

Bumping her bags, Shannon glanced up and down the platform. She'd never seen one so big, with hundreds of people jostling to and fro, all of them in a rush to get somewhere. She'd heard a lot about Glasgow and the busy airport station—not all of it positive—but it was different experiencing it firsthand.

Most of the men, women, and children bustling around her seemed disconnected from their immediate world, tuned in instead to a wider frequency. Cellphone conversations, electronic books, and text messaging all demanded their attention.

Shannon spotted a young mother attempting to navigate the platform, pushing a stroller with a newborn while trying to keep two young children in tow. The little boy was determined to run back toward the trains, while his toddler sister clutching a stuffed bear seemed content to agitate the baby from a sound sleep. Shannon watched the woman's slow progress, tugging at her son and scolding her daughter. To make matters worse, the girl began to cry, hands rubbing at her eyes, and in the process, the stuffed toy slipped from her grasp. Her mother failed to notice, however, and continued on her way. The little girl's cries reached a hysterical pitch when she noticed her bear was missing.

Shannon grabbed her luggage and hurried after the mother. She bent over to pick up the child's toy, and as she did so, she felt her purse wrenched from her shoulder. The force of the pull was so great that it spun her down to the ground. When she got over the initial shock, she jumped up and spotted the thief running away.

She let loose a bloodcurdling scream. "Help! Stop that man! He stole my purse!"

Still clinging to her suitcases, she attempted to run after the man. The thief bumped and jostled people in his path, finally knocking over a man, who seconds before, had been conversing on his cellphone.

"Shannon!" She heard Coleen call out from somewhere behind her.

Two security officers joined her. One continued the pursuit, and the other pulled her aside near a newsstand. "Ma'am, can you tell me what happened?"

Coleen raced to her side as she spoke to the officer.

She pointed in the direction she'd seen the man run. "A man stole my purse. He grabbed it right off my shoulder."

Coleen brought a hand to her mouth in horror. "Oh no."

"Can you describe him?"

"He's wearing a dark blue sweatshirt with a hood. It covered his head so I couldn't see his face."

"What else was he wearing?"

She put her hands to her temples. "Tennis shoes and dark pants, I think."

A tinny voice blared from the security officer's radio. "Subject out of sight. We lost him in the crowd." He plucked it off his duty belt and responded with the description of the man she'd just given.

"Is there any chance I'll get my purse back?" Shannon asked.

The officer shrugged. "We'll do our best, ma'am. What did you have in it?"

"My personal belongings."

"This is a disaster," Coleen moaned. "You can't get through security without your passport. We won't make the flight."

Shannon shook her head. "John used to insist I wear a money pouch around my neck when I traveled with him. Old habits are hard to break, I guess. I've got it on under my clothes. My passport, other identification, credit cards, and cash are in it. And my cellphone is in my pocket."

"Whew," Coleen let out a big sigh.

"But there are other items in my purse I need," Shannon said. "Reading glasses, sunglasses, makeup. And things that are irreplaceable—pictures of my family, for example."

"We'll do what we can," the officer said. "But don't get your hopes up."

He took down her cellphone number and promised to call if they apprehended the man or recovered her purse. Then he left, issuing more orders into his radio.

Shannon looked around and met the gaze of a rotund man working a newsstand nearby. He pulled a toothpick from his mouth. "Welcome to Glasgow, lady."

"It's a good thing you kept your identification and money in that silly bag around your neck," Coleen said.

"Yes, but I just realized something. The letter from the law firm was in the purse. Names, directions ... I don't have any of that memorized."

"I remember one of the names is Barnhill. Or is it Barnwell?"

"That's right, it's Barnwell. And now that I think of it, I believe his office number is logged in my cellphone from when I called him earlier in the week. I'll ring them again and get the information we're missing once we're in the States."

Coleen threw up her hands like she didn't have a care in the world. "So what more do you need? The rest of the items, save for your dear pictures, can be replaced. And come to think of it, even the pictures can be replaced. I'm sure you have the negatives or the digital images."

"I guess, but it'll take a lot of digging through boxes."

"There, you see? We can shop to replace the other items during our layover in New York City. I'm sure there will be plenty of shops in that airport."

Shannon chewed on her lip. She decided the time had come to tell Coleen about the note. "My purse is not the only thing bothering me. I think someone is trying to keep me from going on this trip."

Coleen scoffed. "Why? Because you got mugged in a busy train station? It's unfortunate, but this kind of thing happens every day. You were in the wrong place at the wrong time."

"That's not all. Have you ever had the feeling that someone is following you? I've had it more than once today, and I can't seem to shake it."

"Interesting ... I never would have pegged *you* for a conspiracy theorist," Coleen joked. "You've read too many mystery novels. I think it might be time to switch to a different genre."

"There is one more thing on my mind I need to tell you about. I didn't mention it earlier because, to be frank, I'm not sure what to make of it."

Shannon recounted the story of finding the note outside her door.

Coleen let out a low whistle. "I can see how that might upset you. But let's look at this from a logical perspective. Mrs. Campbell's been leaving bizarre messages on your door for over a week, right?"

"Yes."

"She knew you were planning this trip to Oregon?"

"She did. She insisted on keeping an eye on my plants while I'm gone."

"So there's your answer. For some strange reason, she must have got it in her head you shouldn't go on this trip, so she penned another creepy note and left it on your door. End of story."

"That *is* the most logical assumption." Shannon nodded slowly. "You're probably right."

"Of course I am." Coleen put her arm around Shannon's shoulders and gave her a hug. "Right now, you're under a lot of stress. It's making silly things seem more important than they really are. Trust me."

"Okay. Thank you for putting my mind at ease." Shannon gave herself a mental shake. "Now, let's get going. We have a plane to catch."

* * *

The moment the jet began to taxi down the runway, Shannon felt a twinge of excitement and, right alongside it, a familiar sense of foreboding.

The winds in their little coastal village of Wainscott had a reputation for turning without so much as a moment's notice. Fishermen knew the signs to look for. Their very lives depended on it. A strong wind could carry a boat far out to sea or crash it on a craggy coast.

Her feelings akin to those fishermen, Shannon knew for certain the winds in her life had turned. Though she'd denied it to Coleen's face a week earlier, her heart bore witness to it today. Her life, her destiny, and the answers she longed for lay ahead, in the town of Apple Grove.

She leaned over a sleeping Coleen, lifted the visor covering the window, and looked out. From her high perch, the homes and farmlands were mere squares in a patchwork quilt.

Visions of the sleepy village where she'd grown up washed into conscious thought ... her daily walks across ancient stone bridges, past quaint shops and cobbled streets, and among its verdant foothills, brilliant green and lush. The walks almost always culminated with a climb to the cemetery at the top of the hill, where she'd visit her husband's grave, then her father's, and pull the fresh weeds that had sprung up to claim and cover. Finally, she would rest on the stone bench on the crest of the cliff overlooking the sea. On certain days, sea mists rising off the water sent low clouds to balance on the land, as if heaven itself had touched the earth.

A loud snort interrupted her musings.

She glanced at Coleen, who'd insisted on the window seat. She'd taken her sleeping pills and curled up the moment they'd settled in their seats. The initial snort soon upgraded to full-fledged snoring.

The flight would be long indeed.

Excited at the prospect of meeting her mother's family, Shannon found it hard to sit still as the hours ticked by. She made numerous trips up and down the aisles under the pretense of visiting the loo, trying to burn off nervous energy.

What a stroke of good fortune the seat next to her was free. She couldn't imagine having to carry on a conversation with a complete stranger about why she was going to America. Or squeezing past every time she got up to pace. More than once, she found herself reaching to her neck to grasp the locket. She treasured the link to her past, and she longed to know more.

A few more hours passed before the subtle nuance of the plane's descent signaled their impending arrival.

"Rise and shine, sleepyhead." She shook Coleen's shoulder.

"What?" Coleen slowly opened her eyes, her eyeliner smudged underneath. "Are we in New York already?"

"Yes, thank goodness."

"I didn't snore, did I?"

"Well ..."

Coleen's eyes flew wide open and she looked around, horrified. She lowered her voice to a strangled whisper. "Please tell me I didn't snore on the plane."

"Are you certain you want to know?"

The man in the seat in front of her looked back, an annoyed expression on his face. "You snored all right, lady. Louder than a goose call. Thanks to you, I didn't get a single wink of sleep."

Coleen pulled her blanket off. "I'm so sorry. I took a pill to help me."

"Hmmph," the man muttered, turning back around. "Too bad there's not a pill for snoring."

Coleen made a silly face at the back of his head and then leaned forward in her chair to stretch.

Shannon chuckled. "Awake less than three minutes and causing trouble. I can tell already this trip is going to be quite an adventure."

— 4 —

The Portland airport proved to be miniscule compared to JFK International in New York. The people were dressed in more casual clothing, and the frenetic pace of the other airport was absent.

Shannon and Coleen retrieved their luggage, picked up their rental car, and decided to grab a bite of late lunch in town before the hour's drive to the coast.

"Where shall we eat?" Shannon asked, concentrating hard on her driving.

"It says in this brochure we should visit something called the 'Foodie Trucks' in downtown Portland." Coleen grasped the handle above her shoulder as the car jerked to the right. "Aahh!"

"Sorry. It's going to take some time to adjust to driving on the right side of the road. I'm willing to try a 'Foodie Truck' if you are. Can you figure out how to plug the address into the GPS?"

Less than fifteen minutes later, they stood on Alder Street in downtown Portland before a block-long row of food trucks lit with bright chains of light and tiki torches. The trucks offered everything from *falafels* to Korean-Mexican fusion, to South American *chicharrones* with fried yucca root, to potato *latkes*. Musicians and performance artists entertained. One man swallowed fire, while another juggled fruit. A young woman wearing a baseball cap knelt in the street, sketching a design with sidewalk chalk.

"Look, Coleen, it's three-dimensional." Shannon marveled at the chalk image of a mermaid swimming in the ocean. "The detail is amazing. How can it seem so real?"

They watched the artist for a few minutes and then walked farther up the street. In the end, they chose different food trucks. Shannon glanced at Coleen, who stood one truck over in line behind only a handful of people. She stood behind no fewer than fifteen. By the time she got to the window, she'd made her decision. She ordered curried chicken and potatoes, with eggs and *chapati* bread.

As Shannon placed the order, she looked beyond the server into the kitchen area. A woman in a chef's hat prepared the orders. Something about the woman seemed familiar. Was it her profile? Her stance?

Before she could get a better look at the woman, the server returned to the window and handed her a sales receipt to sign.

"That's a beautiful necklace," the server commented. "It must be an antique."

"Thank you." Shannon signed and picked up her food. "It belonged to my grandmother."

The server moved to the side again, and Shannon glanced back into the kitchen area. The woman in the chef hat was staring straight at her, a slight frown on her face. The moment their eyes met, she looked away.

Shannon heard Coleen call her name. She joined her on a nearby bench. Coleen balanced Czech dumplings with creamy spinach soup on her lap. Since her line had been so much shorter, she was already halfway through her meal by the time Shannon sat down.

"How's your food?" Shannon asked.

"It's delicious. Who would have thought food from a truck could be so delightful?" Coleen held up her spoon. "Do you want to taste it?"

"No, thanks. I can't wait to sink my teeth into this."

Before Shannon could take a bite though, her cellphone rang.

"That must be the kids. I promised to call them when we arrived." She pulled her phone from her new purse and looked at the caller ID. "That's strange, there's no number. Hello?"

"Mrs. McClain?"

"Yes, who am I speaking with?"

"This is Roger Barnwell. I'm calling to find out if you're still planning to attend the reading of Victoria Paisley's will on the eighteenth?"

"I am. In fact, I'll be heading to the Apple Grove Inn shortly."

There was a short pause. "You're in the United States now?"

"Yes. I decided to come in a little early to explore the town and take a look at the store and the estate, if that would be possible. Actually, I'm glad you called, because as luck would have it, my purse was stolen and I've lost—"

Click. The line went dead.

"Hello? Mr. Barnwell?" Frustrated, Shannon hung up.

"Dropped call?" Coleen asked.

"Either that or a very rude attorney. Now let's see ..."

Shannon scrolled through her recently dialed calls until she found the U.S. phone number she'd called earlier in the week. "Aha, I think this is the number." She dialed the law firm.

A woman's voice answered on the second ring. "Barnwell, Meecham and Hanscombe, how may I help you?"

"This is Shannon McClain. I was just speaking with Mr. Barnwell, and I believe we were cut off. Can you put me through to him please?"

There was a slight pause. "Are you certain you were speaking with *Roger* Barnwell?"

"Well, I assume so. He identified himself as such."

"Mr. Barnwell has been tied up in a meeting all afternoon. He hasn't left the boardroom since lunch."

"Perhaps he snuck in a quick call to me? He said he was calling to confirm my attendance at the reading of Victoria Paisley's will on the eighteenth."

The receptionist's tone turned cool. "I can assure you he would not interrupt the meeting he's in to place such a call. I'm the person who usually makes the confirmation calls. In fact, you're on my list to contact. I take it you're planning to attend?"

"Yes, but—"

"Very good, I've made a note. Now, I don't know who called you earlier, but it was *not* Roger Barnwell."

Shannon felt a chill run through her as the receptionist's words sank in. "Thank you."

She ended the call and set her phone down on the bench beside her.

"What's wrong?" Coleen demanded.

"The man who called to find out if I'm still planning to

attend the reading of the will lied to me. He was not Mr. Barnwell."

"Who was he then? And how did he get your number?"

"That's what I'd like to know."

* * *

The drive to Apple Grove was a short one, less than an hour. Thankfully, the beautiful scenery soon took precedence over the strange man's phone call and the women's speculations about its significance.

Once they reached the coastal highway, their route along the coastline was a straight shot. Shannon found it difficult to keep her eyes on the road at times due to the breathtaking rock formations rising from the foam and billow of the ocean.

After a sharp curve that had Coleen clinging, white-knuckled, to her seat cushion, they ascended a long hill and entered the quaint town of Apple Grove. Set slightly inland at a higher elevation, the downtown presented a pleasing array of buildings and shops.

Coleen oohed and ahhed at the charming storefronts. "'Pink Sprinkles'? Why, it's a bakery. We must be sure to pay them a visit while we're here."

"And after that, we can visit Brice's Candy Kitchen down the street," Shannon added. The sign, flanked on two sides by gigantic lollipops, said all that needed to be said about what was inside.

They passed by a variety of stores: T-shirt shops catering to tourists, high-end boutiques, an Italian pizza kitchen, a hat shop, a swimsuit store, a glassblower, seafood restaurants, a beauty salon and spa, a pet grooming shop, and finally, the Paisley Craft Market & Artist Lofts.

Shannon saw a parking space open up right in front. "Come on let's go inside and check it out incognito. We can ask them for directions to the inn."

"All right, but why don't you want to tell the employees who you are?"

"I'd like to get a feel for the place without making anyone else uncomfortable. Does that make sense?"

Coleen shrugged. "You're the boss."

They walked through the wide archway framing the entrance. A young woman sat behind the front counter, reading a book. She greeted them with a brief smile, then quickly returned her attention to her book, never bothering to ask if they needed help. Shannon cringed at the poor customer service, but she let it go for the moment so she could take in the sights around her with a clear mind.

Every inch of the place was stuffed to capacity with craft supplies, fabric, and paints. The beading section featured a large counter containing hundreds of different kinds of beads and findings for making jewelry. Other areas were devoted to knitting, crochet, paper crafts, painting, decoupage, and embroidery. A section devoted to quilting and sewing supplies rounded out the offerings.

"Amazing," Shannon said, drawn to the bead counter. She picked up a pink, opaque bead for a closer examination. "This is Italian glass, made entirely by hand. Do you see the little flower on both sides of the bead? Absolutely stunning."

Coleen took it from her hand and held it up to the light

to admire it. "It's gorgeous. Can you make me a necklace with these?"

"Certainly. I owe you that and much more for coming with me on this trip."

"You don't owe me a thing." Coleen looked around at all the store had to offer. "I'm so happy for you. It's still so hard to believe that all of this is going to be yours."

Shannon noticed a woman teaching a class in the back of the store—stamping and card making from what she could see. She counted eighteen people in attendance.

"I'm pleased to see they offer classes. That should help to bring in repeat customers."

"Mmm-hmm." Coleen stifled a yawn. "Sorry. I think the time change is starting to catch up with me."

"I'm feeling a bit worn down myself. Let's get directions to the inn, check in, and rest for a bit. We can come back later."

"Sounds good."

Ten minutes later, they pulled into a parking lot across from the Apple Grove Inn. A Queen Anne Victorian design, the building was painted buttercup yellow with white trim, set off by a black tiled roof. Its structure appeared to be somewhat elongated, likely due to multiple additions over the years. A historical plaque on the wall indicated the original home had belonged to a steamship captain, and had been built in 1887.

Both women were delighted by the decor they encountered when they entered the threshold. The Victorian theme continued throughout the lobby. Charming settees, conversation chairs, and ottomans, all in pristine condition, were covered and trimmed in fresh fabric and tassels.

The ceilings were painted in delightful frescoes depicting cherubs and clouds, birds, and rainbows. A tearoom beckoned to the right of the foyer. A hand-painted sandwich-board sign indicated it was open for breakfast, lunch, and high tea. Shannon couldn't wait to get a better look at the large collection of teapots displayed on the shelves.

But for now, she needed to stick to the task at hand: check in, call the twins, and recharge. She suspected she would need all of her energy and wits to survive the coming days.

The woman at the front desk had a pleasing look about her. With auburn hair touched by tinges of soft gray, Shannon guessed her to be in her mid-fifties.

"Welcome to the Apple Grove Inn, ladies. My name is Betty Russo. My husband, Tom, and I own the inn. What can I do for you today?"

Coleen made it to the desk first, lugging her heavy suitcase behind her. "We have a reservation."

"Your name?"

"Coleen Douglas."

Betty keyed the name into her computer. "For one week?"

"Yes."

"Wonderful. Are you in town for a special occasion?"

"Oh yes, my friend is here to claim her inheritance. She's about to become the new owner of the craft market down the street."

Shannon glared at her. *Leave it to Coleen to spill the beans.*

"You don't mean the Paisley estate, do you?" As

Betty uttered the words, her eyes focused on the locket at Shannon's throat. Then her gaze moved upwards to Shannon's red hair. "You're Shannon, Victoria's granddaughter from Scotland?"

Shannon blinked. "That's what I've been told."

Betty scurried from behind the desk and gripped Shannon in a full embrace. "It's wonderful to finally meet you." Excitement on her face, she continued. "Victoria spoke of you often. We were close friends, in the same craft circle for many years."

Shannon felt as if the life were being squeezed out of her. "I'm happy to meet you too. I'd love to sit down with you and talk. I have so many questions about my family. Would you have any free time this week?"

"Oh, of course. I'll *make* time for you." Betty brushed away tears. "You're so beautiful. Your red hair is a giveaway. Victoria had red hair when she was young. I've seen pictures of her as a child. You have her eyes, too, almond shaped and lovely. The only difference is hers were green."

Shannon felt hope swell within her. "You knew my grandmother well, then?"

"We were best friends. In truth, she was blessed to have five best friends, but if I were to pick a favorite, I'd say I was the closest to her, though Deborah would clobber me for saying so."

"Deborah?"

"The housekeeper and cook at the estate."

"Is she a part of your craft circle too?"

Betty shook her head. "She's usually busy during our meeting time. If you'd like to talk to the whole gang, our craft circle is meeting tomorrow at the Paisley Craft Market. I'll invite Deborah to come as well. The five of us were very close. I hope you'll come. After all, the store belongs to you now."

Betty's words echoed in Shannon's head: *The store belongs to you now.* The earlier visit to the shop had stirred something within her. Owning a shop like that had been nothing more than a dream before today. Would she really be able to sell the place as she'd planned? She had to admit, part of her hated the idea.

What if the things Coleen had said to her the day she received the inheritance letter were true? That she would get used to living the high life … that she wouldn't return to Scotland. But how could she even entertain the idea of staying in America? That would leave her half a world away from her children, the town she'd grown up in, friends, neighbors, and her *best* friend, Coleen. And yet, she felt the idea planting itself in her mind and in her heart. Though she'd been in the town only a few hours, she couldn't shake the feeling. Apple Grove felt like home.

"You must think I've lost control of my senses." Betty rushed back behind the desk. "Consider yourselves checked in," she announced. "You're on the second floor, room 206. We offer a wonderful breakfast every morning in the tearoom, and for you two girls it's on the house."

"Thank you," Shannon replied. "It was so nice to meet you. I'm looking forward to meeting everyone in your craft circle."

After the women settled into their room, Coleen promptly curled up on her bed and fell asleep. Shannon called the twins to let them know she'd arrived safe and sound and then stretched out on her own bed. Her thoughts soon wandered to the strange phone call she'd received … her stolen purse … and the cryptic note on her door. Although Coleen refused to see any connection, Shannon knew in her gut the events were related.

Someone didn't want her in Apple Grove.

— 5 —

A shrill scream cut through the tranquil silence of the bedroom.

Shannon shot straight up in her bed. "Coleen! Wake up."

"What's that racket?" Coleen mumbled, pulling a pillow off her head.

"It sounded like a woman's scream." Shannon glanced at the clock on her nightstand. It read seven o'clock. They'd slept for three hours. She switched on the lamp by her bed. "I'm going to go see if someone needs help."

"Hold on, I'm coming with you." Coleen staggered from her bed in search of her slippers.

The women stepped out into the hallway and found a small crowd of people gathered outside the room across the hall diagonally from theirs.

They heard a woman yelling inside the room. "Look at this mess. My dress ... it's ruined! What will I wear to Amy's wedding tomorrow? Who would do such a horrible thing?" The woman broke into hysterical sobs.

"I'm so sorry." Shannon heard Betty's strained response. "My husband is downstairs waiting for the police. They should be here any minute. I'm sure they'll get to the bottom of it."

Shannon approached the door to the room and looked inside.

"Oh my," Coleen whispered, peering over her shoulder. Every drawer in the room had been pulled out and the contents dumped onto the floor. Suitcases had also been emptied, their contents cut to pieces.

Two women stood in the center of the mess. One clutched a tattered evening dress in her shaking hand. She glared at Betty. "I demand a refund. I will not sleep here after this. Clearly, this is not a safe place." She waved her free hand in the direction of the mirror over the dresser.

And that's when Shannon saw it.

"Coleen, look," she hissed. "Do you still think my string of bad luck is just coincidence?"

"*LEAVE!*" Coleen paled as she read the word scrawled across the mirror in red lipstick.

"I'm certain this was meant for me," Shannon said. "The intruder got the wrong room."

"Move back and clear a path, please." Two police officers squeezed through the gathering of onlookers and approached the woman holding the tattered dress. "I'm Chief Grayson of the Apple Grove Police Department, and this is Officer Brownley," one of them said.

A little on the heavy side, the chief had brown eyes that matched what remained of his hair. He appeared to be in his early fifties, and, carried himself with confidence. In contrast, the other officer, Brownley, looked to be much younger and unsure of where to stand or what to do. Shannon guessed him to be in his twenties. He might have been considered good looking if not for his jack-o'-lantern teeth.

"Can you tell me what happened?" the chief asked.

The woman clung to the tattered dress and sniffled.

"My sister and I left our room at five o'clock. We walked to the Italian café down the street and ate dinner. Afterward, we strolled around the square for a bit. When we returned this ... *nightmare* is what we found."

Shannon saw Betty standing off to one side, wringing her hands. Their gazes met, and Shannon offered her a supportive smile.

"How long have you both been in town?" the chief inquired.

"Not long. We checked in this afternoon. And I can *assure* you we won't be coming back ..."

Coleen pulled Shannon away from the crowd. "OK, I've given it some thought, and I have to admit your conspiracy theory is starting to look a little less crazy. Perhaps we should tell the police."

Shannon shook her head. "I don't know."

"Listen, you could be in serious danger here. I'm not sure now is the best time to be digging in your heels and insisting on handling this yourself."

Shannon threw up her hands. "If we tell them, they'll probably say the same thing you did. A stolen purse is an everyday occurrence in a crowded train station. And as for the cryptic note? I doubt they'd believe someone followed me all the way from Scotland just so they could write another one on my mirror."

"But what about the phone call?"

Shannon sighed.

"What are you saying? You don't think there's a connection behind it all anymore?" Coleen asked.

"I'm not saying that at all. But I don't know whom I can

trust in this town, and I'm not sure telling the police what I know about this would be of much use to them anyway."

"Do you know something about the break-in?" demanded a deep voice from behind.

The women whirled around to see a dark-haired man standing a few feet away, his blue eyes fixed on Shannon in an intense gaze.

Shannon heard Coleen gulp.

"Are you with the police?" Shannon asked, sidestepping the question. She studied the man's appearance for some clue as to his identity. His attire looked nothing like that of the other policemen—loose-fitting khaki pants, a white shirt, and a black leather jacket.

"Not exactly." Like a cat stalking its prey, he moved closer, and Shannon inhaled the faint scent of his cologne.

She lifted her chin to meet his gaze. "In that case, I'm *not exactly* inclined to tell you anything. If you will excuse us." She grabbed Coleen's hand and pulled her away.

They hadn't made it but a few feet when they heard Betty's voice behind them.

"Michael! Thank you for getting here so fast." She rushed down the hall to join the man who had just questioned Shannon. Her words tumbled out in a frantic stream, "I have two irate guests and the police have no leads. I'm sure our reputation will be sorely damaged by this incident. Oh, the situation is terrible! Can you help us?"

"That depends on the point of entry; we'll review the tapes and see what we can find," he replied. "It's unfortunate, but the system you chose left a few critical areas unmonitored, so we might come up empty."

"Oh no. I was afraid something like this might happen, but Tom was so determined to cut costs at the time."

"However, there might be someone else who can provide us with a lead," Michael added.

Shannon glanced back over her shoulder to find the man staring right at her, his gaze utterly unsettling.

"Shannon?" Betty called out, a confused expression on her face.

Coleen nudged her.

Seeing no other option, Shannon turned and walked slowly toward Betty, thinking about what she should say. She looked from Michael's impassive face to Betty's, which was filled with dismay. Then she switched her focus back to Michael.

The root cause of my newest problem. She narrowed her eyes at him and thought she saw the hint of a smirk forming at the corner of his lips.

"Do you know something about this?" Betty asked her.

"Who is this man?" Shannon demanded, her voice harsher than she'd intended.

"Oh, dear me, where are my manners?" Betty replied. "Shannon, this is Michael Stone, our security consultant. Michael, these are two of our guests, Shannon McClain and her friend, Coleen Douglas."

He extended his hand to Shannon. "It's a pleasure to meet you, Shannon."

"Charmed," she responded, her voice flat.

Michael smiled, revealing perfect white teeth. "So it's true what they say about the Scottish and their tempers."

"W-What?" Shannon sputtered, her irritation rising.

"How would you know where I'm from?"

"Your accent is hard to miss."

Och! Is he making fun of me? Shannon felt her blood pressure rise.

Coleen pushed her way between them and extended her hand. "It's nice to meet you. I'm Coleen."

Michael continued to hold Shannon's hand in a firm grip for another moment as their gazes locked. Then he released her hand and turned his full attention to Coleen.

Betty cornered Shannon at once. "What do you know about the break-in? Did you see something suspicious?"

"No, we didn't." Shannon watched Betty's face fall.

"Did you hear any commotion through the door?"

"Surprisingly, no. We were in our room, but we were asleep."

"So you don't know anything about this?" Betty pressed.

Coleen joined them, lips pursed. Shannon silently willed them to remain shut.

"I'm sorry we can't be more helpful." Shannon felt her stomach turn as she lied. She hated having to do it. "We don't know anything."

"Then why did Michael think you did?" Betty asked.

"I'm not sure." Shannon regarded him sternly; his guarded expression gave away nothing. "Likely it's because he eavesdropped on a *private* conversation and misinterpreted what he'd heard."

"Oh, well, we won't keep you then." Betty said. "I apologize for bothering you, and I do hope this incident hasn't scared you two away."

"Not a chance," Shannon reassured her. "I wouldn't

dream of missing breakfast in your tearoom."

Michael moved directly into her path and held out a business card. "If you should happen to remember anything that might shed light on this situation—"

"Then I'll call the Apple Grove police." Shannon took the card and forced a polite smile.

Coleen coughed nervously and pushed Shannon back toward their room. "What is the matter with you?" she whispered as they moved out of earshot.

"I told you, I don't know whom I can trust in this town yet, so I'm not telling anybody anything. We need to figure a few things out on our own first."

Coleen shook her head. "That's not what I was referring to, but we'll come back to that in a minute. I was talking about your behavior toward that man. That devastatingly *handsome* man, I might add. I've never seen you act that rudely to anyone."

"I don't know. He got under my skin, butting his nose into our business the way he did." Shannon paused. "Was I really that rude?"

Coleen clucked her tongue. "You were an ice queen."

"Oh, honestly."

"Say, did you notice he wasn't wearing a wedding ring?" Coleen gave her an expectant look. "And I'd put him in his mid-forties."

"How lovely for him. And no, I did not notice."

"Admit it. You thought he was handsome."

"I thought nothing of the sort."

"Just admit it. That's why you're acting this way."

Shannon threw up her hands. "Oh, all right, he's a

fine-looking man. A little on the nosy and overbearing side, but handsome. Can we not talk about this anymore?"

Coleen grinned.

Shannon continued. "As I've told you numerous times, I'm not interested in a romantic relationship right now. I wasn't prepared to lose the love of my life, and I'm not sure my heart is ready to take that risk again."

"It's been three years."

"You speak as if my heart should follow some kind of timetable. Maybe other people are like that, but not me."

"Then let's suppose for a minute that you *were* ready. Is he the kind of man you'd be interested in?"

"Absolutely not. Now can we please drop the subject? This isn't a singles cruise we're on, after all. We've come here so I can claim an inheritance and get some answers about my family. Answers I need now more than ever."

"You're right. I'm sorry. I only want to see you happy. Getting back to the topic at hand, you sound like you have a plan. Do you?"

"I do. Tomorrow I intend to ask Betty what she knows about my relatives, including where they live. I think it's time to make a few house calls."

"You think your relatives are behind all this?"

"Yes, unfortunately." Shannon frowned. "Who else would stand to gain from my absence at the reading of Victoria's will?"

"Makes sense."

"What I don't know is how far will they go to get what they want?"

— 6 —

The next morning, Shannon awoke at seven o'clock, a full hour later than the time she usually got out of bed. But considering the jet lag, she figured a little extra sleep wouldn't do her any harm.

Truth be told, she'd awoken because of a nightmare.

In her dream, she was back in the rental car with Coleen, but not for a pleasure ride. Someone was chasing after them in a black truck, with guns trained on their car from the windows. Shannon pressed the gas pedal to the floor to try and outrun the truck, but despite the roar of its overworked motor, the little compact car couldn't pick up any speed. The black truck gained ground quickly. Then, just as it seemed all was lost, she woke up in a panic.

To her surprise, the motor was still running. Heart pumping fast, she followed the direction of the sound.

True to form, Coleen snored in the bed next to her, dead to the world. Shannon had found the source of her dream's sound effects.

Her friend looked a mess. Her hair was in a sleepy tangle, and her arms and legs were splayed in all different directions across the bed. The sheet and blanket hung in a waterfall over the end, and a giant can of hair spray rested on top.

Shannon tiptoed from her bed, showered, and dressed.

In the middle of applying her makeup, she decided to wake her friend.

"Sleepyhead, it's time for breakfast."

Eyes cemented, Coleen lifted her head off the mattress. "Och." Her head fell back against it.

"You wanted to explore the tearoom downstairs, didn't you? The woman we met yesterday, Betty, said our breakfast was 'on the house.' That means it's free."

Coleen's head popped back up, and she managed to pry open one eyelid. "You look nice," she said in a gravelly voice. "Is that new?"

Shannon gave her outfit the once-over in the mirror. A blue skirt with a handkerchief hem, floral print blouse with half sleeves, and a bright blue scarf she'd purchased at a secondhand shop for next to nothing. "No, it's not new. I added some beading to the scarf."

The secondhand scarf now looked high end thanks to the addition of topaz, burgundy, and citrine beads to its thin tassels.

"Smart look for you." Coleen cleared her throat. Rolling to the edge of the bed, she sat up and staggered to the bathroom.

Shannon finished her makeup and flipped on the television to catch the eight o'clock news. A short while later her friend emerged from the bathroom. The fresh smell of soap, shampoo, and hair spray followed her.

"I can't go anywhere," she announced.

"What do you mean?" Shannon picked up the clicker and turned off the television.

Coleen turned her head to the side. A sleep crease ran

along the entire left side of her face. "I have a special pillowcase at home that prevents this."

Hand to her mouth, Shannon fought to suppress a laugh. "Oh, dear." The giggle escaped in spite of her efforts.

"You're laughing? I think I'm creased for life."

"It's not that bad."

Coleen's stomach growled. She looked down at her belly as if betrayed. "Oh, all right, I'm hungrier than I am vain. Let's go."

As they left their room, Shannon did a double take.

"What's wrong?" Coleen asked.

"We *are* staying in room 206, right?"

Coleen looked at the key card in her hand. "That's right."

Shannon's eyes darted to the door of the room that had been ransacked the night before. "Then how can that be room 206 as well?"

"What?"

Shannon and Coleen moved closer for a better look. Shannon touched the brass number on the door. "Look, it's loose. The room number should be 209."

Coleen brought her hand to her mouth. "But that means ..."

"It means we now have proof that whoever broke into this room meant to break into ours."

"What should we do?"

Shannon swallowed. "Nothing, for now. But we need to be on guard. Someone is trying to intimidate me."

"Or worse," Coleen added. "I really think you should take this information to the police."

Shannon shook her head. "Not yet."

"If not now, then when? After someone tries to kill us? I don't know how much more of this I can take."

Shannon placed her hand on Coleen's shoulder. "No one is going to kill us. They surely would have tried by now if that was their intent. Whoever is trying to scare us off will soon realize we don't scare easily and give up. After the reading of the will, I'm sure the antics will stop. We're going to be fine."

Coleen chewed on her lip. "OK, I guess. I'm starving. I can't think straight when I'm this hungry."

"Let's go."

The two headed downstairs to the tearoom and settled into a pink upholstered booth. Sweet pea blossoms clustered in a milk glass vase adorned their table. Shannon noticed that the salt and pepper shakers at each table were different. Theirs were a pair of ceramic garden snails in a cream and floral design.

"Pssst, there's Betty," Coleen whispered. "She's headed this way."

"Good. I'd like to get an early start picking her brain about my family."

"There you girls are." Betty greeted them with a joyful expression. "How are you? I hope the events of the evening didn't keep you from a good night's sleep."

"Not at all," Shannon assured her.

Coleen agreed, and then self-consciously launched into a lengthy explanation about her sleep crease.

"Did the police catch the vandal?" Shannon interjected when Coleen took a breath. "I'm afraid not." Betty wore her hair in an attractive updo. A pair of stunning emerald-and-diamond earrings dangled from her ears. "I fear we'll never know who was behind it or why."

"Your earrings are lovely," Coleen remarked.

"Thank you. They're a gift from my husband. Yesterday was our anniversary."

"Oh, no," Coleen said. "I hope the break-in didn't completely ruin your celebration."

"I have to admit, it put a damper on it. But we've survived a lot worse over the years." She winked. "We managed to salvage some time together."

"How many years?"

"I've been married thirty-five wonderful years to the man I love."

A touch of sadness caught at Shannon's heart. She forced a smile. "You must be so happy."

Betty nodded. "May I sit down with you girls?"

"Please do." Coleen invited.

A waitress wearing a pink-and-white-checkered uniform arrived at the table. Once Betty was seated, she passed out paper menus shaped like teapots.

"Aren't these darling?" Coleen said.

"The two breakfast specials today are homemade croissants with fresh strawberries and melon, or egg-and-sausage bake, with toast points and marionberry jam," the waitress said.

"What do you recommend?" Shannon asked Betty.

"The Tea Breakfast is our most popular."

"Then I'll have that." Shannon handed her menu back to the waitress.

"Make that two," Coleen said.

"Why don't you bring us a pot of English Breakfast tea first, Livvy?" Betty instructed the waitress. "And there's no charge for the meals."

Livvy stuck her pad back in her pocket and her pencil behind her ear, and nodded to Betty. "You're the boss."

She returned a few moments later with a pot of tea covered by a quilted teapot cozy that jingled as she set it in the middle of the table. Shannon admired the tiny brass bells sewn to the handle.

The waitress placed a unique teacup and saucer in front of each lady. "I'll have your breakfast out in a few minutes."

As the tea steeped, Betty began to tell them about her craft group, the Purls of Hope.

"As I mentioned yesterday, I've known Victoria for many years." Betty said. "We store owners all know one another in this town. We try and look out for one another."

She removed the tea cozy to reveal a whimsical teapot with an Alice in Wonderland theme.

"What was she like?" Shannon asked, impatient to learn more.

Before Betty could answer, Livvy returned and set a small plate before each of them, each with a clutch of scrambled eggs and two tiny sausages.

"This looks wonderful," Coleen exclaimed, her attention focused on the food.

Livvy returned a scant minute later with a three-tiered silver server. It was laden with delectables, stacked and tucked on every inch of the tiers—cream scones, miniature carrot muffins, strawberries filled with piped-in cream, toast points, pumpkin bread, biscuits, banana bread, and raspberry tarts.

Betty bowed her head and said a blessing before they began to eat.

"Now, to answer your question, Shannon. How can I describe your grandmother in one sitting?" Eyes misty, Betty contemplated. "For starters, she had a huge heart. Victoria gave generously to charities, especially those for orphans and people suffering from illnesses. She was a very talented artist. I can't think of any craft she couldn't master once she put her mind to it."

"Did she bead?" Shannon asked.

"She did." Betty thought for a moment. "She had a wonderful sense of humor too. I'd say she was the prankster of the group. She loved puzzles and riddles, and she usually had her nose in a mystery book when she wasn't crafting."

"Sounds a bit like someone I know," Coleen said, giving Shannon a pointed look.

"She also collected unique works of art, sculptures mostly. You'll find a rather eclectic collection throughout her mansion."

"She told you she planned to will it to me?"

Betty smiled. "We didn't keep too many secrets from each other in our little group."

"Did she ever speak of my mother?" Shannon held her breath, bracing herself for the answer.

Betty's smile faded. "Not very often. Beth was the one topic Victoria tended to avoid, with everyone."

Shannon fought to keep her disappointment in check.

"However, she did speak of you often," Betty added.

"She loved you very much."

"It's so odd to hear you say that," Shannon said. "I knew nothing about her until a week ago."

Betty nodded. "I can imagine how overwhelming all of this must be for you."

"It's been emotionally draining, that's true," Shannon sighed. "Even though Victoria rarely spoke about my mother, do you at least know if she's still alive? Or when the last time Victoria spoke to her might have been?"

Betty shook her head. "I really can't say."

"Do you have any idea how long Victoria lived at the mansion?"

"As far as I know, she lived there her entire married life. And then all of her widowed life as well."

"So that would mean my mother grew up in that house," Shannon said.

"What about other relatives?" Coleen asked, spreading a generous portion of lemon curd on a hot scone. "Did Victoria have any other children besides Beth?"

"No, Beth was her only child. But Victoria did have two younger sisters. They're both still alive as far as I know."

Shannon and Coleen exchanged glances.

"Do they live in Apple Grove?" Shannon asked.

"Nadine, the youngest sister, lives in Portland. She's a widow and never had any children. Barbara lives with her husband somewhere between here and Portland. Their kids and grandkids reside in the area as well." Betty paused to sip her tea. "You must be excited at the prospect of meeting your maternal relatives after all of these years. What an interesting reunion that will be."

"Interesting indeed," Coleen quipped.

"Would you be so kind as to give me their last names and any other information you have that could help me get in touch with them?" Shannon asked.

"Of course."

"And would it be too much trouble to get directions to Victoria's estate? I had a letter with the address on it, but it was stolen, along with my purse."

"You poor dear," Betty said. "It's no trouble at all."

"Thank you."

"And thanks again for this delicious breakfast," Coleen added. "You have a fabulous chef."

"I have to agree with you; our baker *is* extraordinary. But then, it's no surprise. She's related to your cook." Betty winked at Shannon.

Shannon blinked. "My cook?"

"Yes, Deborah."

"Oh, right. At the mansion."

"Her sister, Gertrude, does all of our baking." Betty slid out of the booth. "I'll go see if I can find contact information for your relatives. Be back in a few minutes."

"Wonderful."

Filled with disappointment at the lack of answers about her mother and trepidation about meeting her relatives, Shannon sipped the last of her tea in quiet reflection, replaying in her mind all that Betty had revealed about Victoria.

Unable to resist talking for too long, Coleen soon broke the silence. "Your grandmother's friend is nice."

"She seems to be."

"*Seems* to be? What do you mean by that?"

"I still don't know whom I can trust in this town. So I'm being careful not to trust anyone yet. Not even Betty."

Coleen lifted a ripe strawberry to her mouth. "I understand what you're saying, but figuring Betty as a suspect? That seems a little cynical, not at all like the friend I know."

"The friend you knew a few days ago was poor as a church mouse. Now she's on the verge of becoming *nouveau riche*, and she has no idea what to do with any of it."

A puzzled look crossed her friend's face. "Are you considering a move to America now?"

Shannon played with her napkin, pulling and threading it through her fingers. "Not permanently. But I feel like there are answers to important questions about my life here, pieces of history that I'm meant to discover. I'm not sure I'll be able to do so in a short week or two."

"I think I would feel the same way if I were in your shoes."

Shannon shrugged. "Much will depend on how the next few days go, of course."

They fell silent as Betty returned with a slip of paper in hand. She handed it to Shannon. "Nadine's information was easy to find, but I had to ask for a little assistance in obtaining Barbara's. I called Michael, the security consultant you met last night, remember?"

"He's a hard man to forget."

Coleen snorted at her friend's tone, inhaling powdered sugar in the process. She began to cough and reached for her tea.

Betty failed to notice the sarcasm in Shannon's voice. "He was able to look up the address on the spot."

"It helps having friends in the right places." Coleen offered, tears in her eyes from her coughing fit.

Betty continued. "He was even kind enough to offer to accompany you today if you'd like. He thought it might help to have someone with you who knows the area well. You don't want to get lost trying to find your way. The roads off the main highway can be a little tricky."

Shannon gritted her teeth. *The egotistical man! What kind of an idiot does he think I am?* She assumed a facial pose that she hoped would pass for a smile. "Such a thoughtful offer. Please tell him thank you, but we'll manage just fine on our own. Our car has GPS."

"Will do. I'd better get back to the front desk. It looks like we're getting busy out there. You ladies have a wonderful day. Will I see you tonight at our craft circle?"

"I wouldn't miss it for the world. What time?"

"Five o'clock."

"We'll be there," Shannon said.

Betty left their table and strolled out of the room.

Coleen sat back, leaning her head against the booth. "Getting back to our conversation, if I were you, I wouldn't give leaving Scotland a second thought. If the attorney's letter was correct, you're going to inherit a home without a mortgage and all the property around it. What is it? Fifteen acres? Think about all that land. Not to mention you'll also own a business that's tailor-made for you—a gigantic craft store."

"It all sounds too good to be true, doesn't it? I still feel like I'm in a dream."

"It's a once-in-a-lifetime opportunity, that's for certain.

Cryptic threats and phone calls aside, I don't know why you wouldn't consider staying here."

"What about my children?"

"They love you and want to see you happy." Coleen rested her arms on the table. "The fact is, your children are grown. They'll be moving off soon to start their own lives. In a few short years, they'll likely fall in love and get married. Who knows where they'll move? But you can be certain they'll visit you wherever you go."

"I suppose that's true."

"And," Coleen's voice caught, "even though I will miss you in the worst way, I'll take solace in knowing you're truly happy, and not pinching every penny or staying up nights worrying about how you're going to pay your bills."

The sight of tears welling in her friend's eyes wrenched Shannon's heart. "I can handle most of what life throws at me, but I can't handle seeing you cry."

"I can't help it."

"How could I leave you and the life I have back home?"

Coleen leaned forward to grasp her friend's hands across the table. "As difficult as it is to accept, your life changed the day you lost John. You've been floundering ever since, looking for purpose and direction, unwilling to move on. But I tell you, Shannon McClain, deep down, you're the strongest, most innovative woman I know. I'd have keeled over and given up in your place, but you didn't—you survived. Now it's time to move beyond basic survival and make a life for yourself."

She knew Coleen was right. The time had come for her to break free from the emotional holding pattern she'd been in for the past three years. As much as she loved her friend, she couldn't shake the feeling they'd soon be parting ways to embark upon separate journeys in life.

She was overcome with emotion at the realization. She simply couldn't bring herself to declare out loud what her heart already knew.

Shannon turned away to keep her friend from seeing her own tears. "Come on. Let's go see if we can shake up my family tree. Maybe we can find out who's behind all of the nonsense."

7

Coleen let out a low whistle. "I can't believe *this* is going to be yours."

"Nor can I," Shannon replied, absently fingering the locket around her neck.

Still seated in their rental car, the women stared in awe at the Mediterranean-style mansion before them. Semicircular tiers of stone steps, wide and inviting, led to the front door. Its walls were finished in putty-hued stucco. Terra-cotta tiles adorned the roof. Decorative turrets on the front corners of the structure added to the home's impressive stature.

"If my calculations are correct, it's got three levels." Coleen said. "Perhaps four if there's a basement. No wonder your grandma needed a housekeeper."

Everywhere she looked, Shannon found something pleasing to the eye. She relished the ornamental rose garden flanking the home to the right and longed to walk the graveled path next to it to explore all the plantings. She admired the balcony with white stone balustrades on the second floor and a smaller version on the third floor.

Magnificent. She thought about her mother and what it must have been like for her to grow up in a house so grand.

"Shall we go knock on the door and see if your housekeeper is in?" Coleen shook her head. "Goodness, I'll never get used to hearing myself say that to you."

"I daresay I'll never get used to hearing it." Shannon got out of the car and headed for the steps.

They rang the bell multiple times but received no response.

"Perhaps the bell is broken." Coleen banged on the massive door with her fist.

After a few minutes, they gave up and turned back toward the car. Ahead of them, an older couple approached, shuffling carefully up the drive.

"Betty didn't mention Deborah had a husband, did she?" Shannon asked.

"Not that I heard."

"Good morning," the woman called out.

Shannon and Coleen walked down the drive to greet them.

"I don't believe we've met," the woman said. "I'm Tippy and this is Wyatt. We live across the lane a ways down. Victoria's drive is part of our usual morning stroll. It helps us to avoid walking on the main road. I hope we're not bothering you."

"Not at all," Shannon replied.

"We're really going to miss her around here." Tippy's expression grew somber. "Are you a relative?"

"Are you blind?" the elderly man next to her barked. "Of course she's related. She looks just like her."

"Mind your manners, Wyatt," Tippy scolded. She took a closer look at Shannon. "I suppose she resembles Victoria somewhat."

"Not Victoria—the girl." The man scrutinized Shannon from head to toe, squinting as he did. "Beth."

"You knew my mother?" Shannon asked, filled with hope once again that she might get some answers.

"Of course," Tippy interjected. "We've lived here for over fifty years. And now that you mention it, Wyatt, she does look a bit like Beth."

The old man turned and began to shuffle away. "Got to keep moving or I'll run out of steam before we make it home. Tell Beth I said hello. I didn't get the chance to talk to her the last time I saw her. I wanted to congratulate her on her article. It's sure to stick a bee in somebody's bonnet."

"What article? Wait!" Shannon hurried forward to catch up to him. "Are you saying you've seen her recently?"

He stopped. "Sure, I saw her last—"

"Wyatt! Hush," Tippy interrupted. "Don't go telling stories to this nice young woman."

"I'm not telling stories." Frustrated, Wyatt waved his hand in the air and started to walk away again.

"Please accept my apologies if he's upset you." Tippy lowered her voice. "Wyatt's memory has started to fail. He doesn't always know what year it is. Or who he saw doing what."

"Oh, I see," Shannon said, utterly deflated.

"He asked me this morning if I'd remembered to let Daisy out. She was our dog, she died over twenty-five years ago."

"I'm so sorry. That must be an awful thing to watch."

Tippy smiled. "It's not easy. But no matter what, he's still my dear Wyatt, my 'true north.' Even if he doesn't always know which way north is." She looked down the drive. "I'd better catch up to him before he gets away. It was nice to meet you both."

"You too," Shannon said.

"Wyatt, slow down." Tippy muddled after him, gaining on him by degrees.

"It's like watching a race in slow motion," Coleen remarked. "What an adorable couple."

"I don't know how much more of this emotional roller coaster I can take," Shannon blurted, brushing her hair back from her face. "I think we've learned all we can here. Let's pay a visit to my Great-Aunt Nadine."

Coleen put an arm around her friend's shoulders and together they walked back to the car.

Shannon took one last look up at the mansion before sliding into her seat. As she did so, something caught her eye. "Did you see that?"

"See what?"

"The curtains on the third-floor window. They moved."

Coleen eyes grew wide. "Are you certain?"

"Yes. I think someone was watching us."

* * *

"It would appear your entire family is filthy rich," Coleen stated as they approached the front door of a Portland mansion that looked to be every bit as large as Victoria's.

"Shh. Someone might hear you," Shannon warned.

"You still haven't told me what you plan to say to this great-aunt of yours. Are you going to come right out and ask her if she's trying to chase you out of town so she can have your inheritance? Because I don't think that's going to work."

"SHHHH!" Shannon hissed. "I haven't decided yet. At the very least, I want them all to know I'm not frightened by their tactics. And that I'm not going anywhere." She reached out and rang the doorbell.

"Can I just go on the record as saying *I'm* more than a little frightened by their tactics at this point?" Coleen murmured.

"Hush. I hear someone coming."

The door swung open, and a petite woman who looked to be in her seventies stood before them. "May I help you?"

"Hello. Are you Nadine?"

Nadine's gaze shifted from Shannon to Coleen and back again. "Yes. How can I help you ladies?"

"I'm Shannon McClain, Victoria Paisley's granddaughter. And this is my good friend Coleen."

Shannon watched the older woman's expression change from one of confusion to recognition.

Nadine put a hand to her mouth. "Oh my word, I should've known just by looking at you. The resemblance to your mother is striking."

"You're the second person to tell me that today."

Before Shannon could react further, Nadine reached across the threshold and embraced her in a hug. She had a surprisingly strong grip for a woman of her age and build. "I'm so happy to finally meet my great-niece."

When she pulled away, Shannon saw tears in the woman's eyes. Any suspicion that Nadine might have had something to do with recent events all but vanished. "It's nice to meet you too. I have so many questions about the family. I hope you can provide some answers."

"Of course, dear. I'll tell you anything you wish to know," Nadine said. "But I'm afraid it can't be today. I'm on my way out the door. My good friend's husband passed away, and I'm running late for his funeral. Could we talk tomorrow, or perhaps later this week?"

"That would be wonderful. I'll be in the area for a while, so whenever it is convenient for you."

"Where are you staying?" Nadine asked.

"At the Apple Grove Inn."

"Then why don't I come to you instead of you driving all the way back here? We can meet for dinner near the inn. I'll call you tomorrow. What's the best way to reach you?"

Shannon gave Nadine her cellphone number and they said their goodbyes.

"I can't see her being involved in any of this, can you?" Coleen asked once they were back in the car.

"To be honest, no. I'm really looking forward to having dinner with her."

"So that leaves your other great-aunt, Barbara, as the most likely suspect."

"Or someone in her family. Betty said she has kids."

"True." Coleen punched an address into the GPS system. "Let's go talk to Barbara and see what we can find out, shall we?"

Two hours later, they still had not arrived at their intended destination.

"Where are we?" Shannon fumed, making her third U-turn in less than thirty minutes.

"I don't know, but I've got to use the loo," Coleen whined. "All I see are trees, trees, and more trees."

"Are you sure you entered the correct address into the GPS?"

"Positive," Coleen snapped.

Shannon sighed. "Well, I give up. We're running out of time. I don't want to miss the craft circle meeting this evening at the store. Let's head back to the inn."

"Sounds good. Which way is 'back to the inn'?"

"I have no idea."

"There went my hope of finding a bathroom soon." Coleen tapped her finger against her chin, pretending to ponder. "You know, I recall *someone* trying to warn us about the very situation we now find ourselves in. Now, who was that?"

"Don't start."

"I can't understand why you dislike Michael so much. You don't even know him."

"I don't dislike him. I dislike the way he continually tries to butt into my business."

"He's remarkably handsome."

"So you've pointed out."

"And I'm ninety-nine percent sure he's single."

"Coleen," Shannon warned.

Her friend raised her eyebrows. "I'm simply making observations."

"His handsomeness, his singleness, all of it is a moot point because I doubt our paths will even cross again."

Coleen wrinkled her nose. "In a town the size of Apple Grove? I wouldn't be so sure."

— 8 —

The walk to the craft store was a quiet one, but after the day she'd had, Shannon didn't mind. Even Coleen seemed to enjoy the silence as she strolled beside her.

The setting sun bathed the downtown square in long shadows. A few children lingered around a bubbling fountain in the town square garden, squeezing the last few minutes of playtime out of the day. The light in a wrought iron lamppost clicked on as Shannon passed, reminding her that evening was fast approaching. *Just one more night before the reading of the will, then perhaps all of the nonsense will stop.*

She cast a discerning eye at the worn façade of the store as they approached. The paint was chipped and faded, the sign outdated. Two topiary plants flanking the main entrance had lost their shape; both were badly in need of a trim and a good watering. It was clear the manager had let things go. From the dismal look of things on the outside, Shannon wondered how much the manager had let things go on the inside. Had she bothered to keep up with regular inventories? Were the books balanced?

After the reading of the will, her first order of business would be to inventory all the merchandise and comb through the books.

"According to the business hours posted in the window,

the store should be open now," Coleen commented. "I wonder why the sign is flipped to 'Closed'?"

"That *is* strange." Shannon pulled on the door and it opened.

As they entered the shop, a tiny bell above them heralded their arrival. The shop appeared to be completely empty except for Betty, who emerged from the back of the store at the sound of the tinkle.

"You're right on time, ladies. I'm so glad you're here." With a smile on her face, she locked the door behind them.

Shannon looked around, puzzled. "Shouldn't the store be open for business now?"

"Yes, but I'm following your grandmother's instructions. I made a promise."

"Is the manager here?"

Betty shook her head. "We sent her away. She'll be back in an hour. Follow me. Everyone is anxious to meet you."

"But I don't understand ..."

Betty put her arm around Shannon's shoulders. "Please, the others are waiting."

In the back of the store, past the knitting supplies, was a cozy corner. A collection of club chairs in a pink paisley print faced a low round table in the center. In each of the chairs sat a woman, her grandmother's closest friends.

The women stood when she and Coleen entered.

"Ladies," Betty said, gesturing to Shannon. "This is Victoria's granddaughter, Shannon McClain, who has come to our fair town all the way from Wainscott, Scotland."

Much to Shannon's surprise, they began to clap.

"And the beautiful woman standing next to her is her

best friend, Coleen." They clapped for her as well.

"Shannon, I present to you the Purls of Hope along with Deborah, Victoria's long-time friend, live-in housekeeper, and cook." Betty nodded at a white-haired woman who appeared to be in her late fifties. "Deborah is not a regular member of the group. But she agreed to come and help us explain a few things to you."

Shannon's heart raced. *Finally, some answers.*

The first to approach, a full-figured woman with a stylish platinum-blond bob, extended her hand. "I'm Joyce Buchanan, and I'm so happy to finally meet you, Shannon."

"Pleased to make your acquaintance as well."

Joyce adjusted a slinky row of sparkly bangle bracelets on her wrists. "I own Pink Sprinkles Bakery here in town. I hope you'll come by and visit while you're here."

Coleen interjected, "We saw that on the way in. I wanted to stop in the moment we arrived."

Joyce let out a full, hearty laugh. "I'd love to have you girls sample some of my favorite pastries. I make a mean red velvet cupcake."

A younger woman approached next. Shannon guessed her to be in her thirties. "I'm Kate Ellis. I own Ultimutt Grooming. If you saw the bakery, you saw my place. We're right next door."

"There's a picture of a poodle in a bathtub on the sign, right?" Shannon recalled.

"That's right." The woman smiled, revealing Cupid's-bow lips and even rows of beautiful white teeth. She wore little makeup, and her long brown hair was pulled back into a single braid.

"I love your T-shirt," Coleen remarked. The shirt featured a dachshund along with the phrase, "Want to see tricks? Get a poodle."

Kate looked down. "Oh, this ... I bought it at a grooming convention. And yes, there are such things as pet grooming conventions."

The only Purl she hadn't met yet moved to join them. She had a gentle grace about her that made a favorable impression on Shannon.

"Hello. I'm Melanie." She extended her hand.

Large green eyes peered at Shannon from behind petite gold-rimmed glasses. Melanie wore pale blue linen pants, wrinkled in places from sitting, and a matching buttoned-up blouse. Flecks of gray peppered her wavy black hair, which was cut in a short bob.

Betty put an arm around her. "Melanie is recovering from breast cancer." She squeezed her closer. "She's our inspiration."

"I'm so sorry to hear that. Are you feeling well now?" Shannon asked.

Melanie smiled. "I finished my last round of treatment about five months ago and have been pronounced cancer free. I have a follow-up appointment with the doctor next week. We'll see if he continues to give me a clean bill of health."

"That's what we're all praying for," Betty said.

"Amen to that!" Joyce added.

"But enough about that," Melanie said. "I work part time at The Flower Pot florist shop. You may have seen the shop on Main Street. Sometimes I helped your grandmother here as well."

"Do you have children?" Shannon asked.

"Yes." Her face softened. "I have a son, Greg. He lives in Portland."

Betty spoke up. "Now that we've all met, why don't we have a seat?" Two padded folding chairs had been brought in to accommodate the extra women, one for Deborah and one for Coleen. The already-tight space was cramped with the additional chairs, but Shannon managed to squeeze into the circle and take a seat in one of the club chairs as directed; Coleen sat beside her. Once everyone was seated, Betty gave Shannon and each of the Purls a basket with a black slate attached. A name was written in chalk on each slate.

Deborah and Coleen did not have baskets, but Kate offered to get them the craft materials of their choice if they wanted to join in.

The basket passed to Shannon had her grandmother's name on it. It contained a rich burgundy yarn with green steel knitting needles. She pulled out the unfinished project and held it up for inspection—a beautiful scarf of intricate design.

"Victoria was knitting that piece when she got sick," Betty explained. "We took the circle to her house when her heart failure progressed to the point that she was unable to come here."

"It's exquisite." Shannon admired the beautiful yarn and expert workmanship.

"To give you a little more background about the group, Melanie is the reason we started meeting," Betty said.

All eyes turned to Melanie, who sat with her legs coiled in the confines of the chair. She smiled in response.

Betty continued: "A little over a year ago, when we heard Melanie had breast cancer, well, it was awful news. We all wanted to help her, but we didn't know how to be of much use. Then, when her husband walked out on her shortly after the diagnosis, we knew we had to do something to help get her back on her feet, financially and emotionally. So we formed the Purls of Hope. Our original goal was to knit items to sell so we could help her pay her medical bills. Victoria donated the yarn. Even though Melanie's on the mend now, we still get together to knit and socialize."

"None of us wanted to stop meeting," Joyce joined in. "Now we make chemo caps and lap blankets for cancer patients. We also craft other items as well to raise money for research. Victoria continued to donate most of the yarn and other supplies. When we needed more expensive yarns, she'd sell it to us at a fraction of the cost. She was a very generous woman."

Shannon trained her eyes on Melanie. "I can't believe your husband would leave you at a time like that. What a horrible thing to do."

Melanie tugged at her yarn as she spoke. "He said he couldn't deal with the whole thing ... the sickness, the treatment. He didn't want a sick wife, plain and simple. So he left."

Coleen shook her head. "That must have been devastating for you."

"None of us could believe it," Kate remarked. "I mean, who *does* that sort of thing?"

"Tell us about yourself, Shannon," Joyce urged, attempting to change the subject. "We want to know all about you."

Trying not to let her nerves get the best of her, Shannon cleared her throat. "There's not much to say. I've lived in Scotland all of my life. I married a Scotsman. I have two children, Alec and Lara. They're twins, both in college now. My husband died in an automobile accident three years ago. Last week, I received a letter informing me Victoria Paisley was my maternal grandmother, and so now ... I'm here."

Before anyone could comment or ask another question, she continued: "If you don't mind, part of the reason I've come on this trip is to learn all that I can about the family I never knew. Would it be OK if we talk about Victoria and my other relatives?"

The ladies shared knowing looks.

"Of course." It was Betty who spoke up. "As you might have gathered from our conversations, your grandmother was well known and loved in this town. Everyone knew Victoria. She never met a stranger. How else to best describe her?"

"Very social."

"Gregarious."

Joyce and Kate's words overlapped one another.

Melanie rose from her chair. "Be right back." She left the corner.

Betty continued, "As I mentioned this morning, she had no other children besides your mother, Beth. The only family members she had left in the area were her two sisters."

"Barbara and Nadine," Shannon said. "I met Nadine today. We didn't get to talk for very long, but we plan to meet for dinner this week."

"Did you meet Barbara as well?" Betty inquired.

"No. We'd stopped by Victoria's estate first, and by the time we finished with Nadine it was getting to be too late."

"Getting lost in the wilderness ate up a lot of our time too," Coleen added.

Shannon glared at her.

"Did you say you were at the house today?" Deborah demanded, her voice gruff.

"Yes, we rang the bell, but there was no answer." Shannon watched the woman's expression, recalling the movement she'd seen in the third-floor window of the mansion as they left.

"That's because I was out. If I'd known you were coming, I would have planned to be there." Deborah's expression was hard. Shannon began to wonder how her grandmother could've found her to be a friendly companion for so many years.

"Do you still plan to contact Barbara?" Kate asked.

"Yes. Betty mentioned she has a husband, children, and grandchildren?"

Shannon noticed Joyce shift nervously in her seat.

"Trevor is her husband," Betty said. "He's a few years her senior. They have two sons, who would be your second cousins, Keith and Fitz. Both boys are married and have grown children of their own."

"Is that it?"

"If you knew them, you'd be asking 'Isn't that enough?'" Deborah muttered.

"Oh dear." Joyce picked up the scarf from her basket and made a pretense of checking the needles to make certain none of the loops had slipped off.

Shannon turned to Deborah. "Why do you say that?"

"If you stick around long enough, you'll understand."

"None of us is perfect, and we certainly don't wish to disparage your family in any way," Joyce blurted. "But our dealings with some of them, and your grandmother's dealings with them, have been ... disappointing."

Shannon watched her struggle to find the right words. Joyce finally gave up and motioned to the housekeeper. "Deborah should be the one to elaborate. She knows the situation better than any of us."

"Are you all trying to say that my relatives—Nadine excluded—are pretty much a collection of unsavory characters?" Shannon asked.

"Yes," Deborah said, "I'm afraid so."

Betty chimed in quickly: "Shannon, we didn't mean for you to get the impression that we're untrustworthy or trying to be deceptive in any way. Believe me, it's like walking on eggshells, trying to answer your questions in a fair way without saying anything that might turn you against the only family you have left."

Deborah cleared her throat. "To give you a little background, Trevor used to be in shipping. Not like your grandfather, James, though. Trevor had some kind of international import business. His sons took it over when he retired."

Shannon planted her elbows on the arms of the chair. "Go on."

"The business is a flop. Always has been. The boys don't know what they're doing, and Trevor barely kept it afloat when he ran it. So where do you suppose they got their money?"

"Victoria?"

"That's right. They're a bunch of money-grubbers, always coming to your grandmother with some kind of sob story, business venture, or medical expense."

The room went silent.

Kate spoke up, "Keith and Fitz were the worst. Those two were a constant drain on her. We all saw what was going on."

"We told her as much," Betty added. "But she continued to fund them, in spite of what we said. She told us she had her reasons."

Joyce folded her arms. "If you ask me, I think they had her over a barrel. Who knows? Maybe blackmail. But then I can't imagine her ever doing anything worthy of blackmail. The woman was a perfect jewel."

"Now that Victoria is gone, it will be interesting to see how they manage to survive without her money," Betty said.

"They'll hatch a new scheme, I'm sure," Deborah said.

Shannon and Coleen exchanged a meaningful look. Shannon suspected that scheme involved chasing her out of town so she would default on her inheritance and they could all split it. It saddened her to realize they would never welcome her into the family with loving arms.

Melanie returned to the group bearing a tray of coffee, cups, sugars, and cream. A brown paper package was tucked under one arm. "Sorry, girls. I planned to make marionberry muffins this morning, but I ran out of time."

"What else can we tell you about your grandmother, Shannon?" Betty asked. "I know you must have a million questions."

Shannon sighed. "I do. But as you might expect, the person I'd really like to know more about is my mother. What she was like, what her interests were—anything at all."

"Your father didn't tell you those kinds of things?" Kate asked.

"No. He wouldn't discuss her."

"Unfortunately, none of us knew Beth," Betty said. "And, like I told you at breakfast, she was the one topic Victoria didn't discuss."

"Beth was a journalist," Deborah stated. All eyes turned to her.

Shannon leaned forward in her chair, recalling what the old man had said about reading her article. "Do you know whom she wrote for?"

Deborah shook her head. "I wish I could tell you."

Shannon looked around at the ladies in the circle. They seemed so genuine and kind. They reminded her of her Crafternoon circle back home. She was beginning to understand why Victoria had trusted and relied on them.

"That's OK. You've told me she was a journalist, and that's more than I knew before. Thank you." Shannon smiled at them. "You are all so kind to meet with me tonight and welcome me into your circle."

Betty lifted her scarf. "We'd better get busy knitting. These scarves aren't going to knit themselves."

"Aren't we forgetting something?" Melanie signaled Betty with a tilt of her head and furrowed brow.

"Oh! Of course, how could I forget the very reason for this special meeting?"

Melanie set the brown paper package on the table in

front of Shannon. "Victoria made this for you. She instructed us to give it to you if you chose to come to Apple Grove after her passing."

Shannon carefully unwrapped the paper, wondering what it could be. *Definitely something framed.* She could feel the curves of the wood. She pulled the last bit of paper away to reveal an exquisite needlepoint, an intricate Celtic cross in blue, twined with roses.

"A Blessing for a New Home," Shannon read aloud.

"Will you please read it to all of us?" Betty asked.

"All right.

> ***'Blessing For A New Home***
> *A blessing upon your new home,*
> *A blessing upon your new hearth,*
> *A blessing upon your new dwelling,*
> *Upon your newly kindled fire,*
> *A blessing upon your tallest grass,*
> *A blessing upon your spouse,*
> *A blessing upon your growing son,*
> *Upon your growing daughter,*
> *A blessing upon the household's helpers,*
> *A blessing upon the children yet unborn,*
> *A blessing upon wise parents,*
> *Upon the work of your hands,*
> *A blessing upon your goods and income,*
> *A blessing upon your kith and kin,*
> *A blessing upon you in light or darkness*
> *Each day and night of your lives.'"*

Coleen leaned over to look at it. "It's beautiful."

"Brings tears to my eyes," said Joyce.

"This needlepoint was the last thing she made," Melanie said. "And it gave her great pleasure to stitch it for you."

Shannon set it on her lap, overcome with emotion. "I adore it."

For the next hour, the group knitted happily together, relating humorous stories about Victoria. Coleen shared the story about her sleep crease, much to their amusement. In spite of the recent upheavals in her life, Shannon found herself having a relaxed and pleasant time with the Purls.

She was surprised at how comfortable she felt with a group of women she barely knew. So comfortable, in fact, that she almost forgot she was thousands of miles from home.

— 9 —

As the craft meeting ended and the Purls dispersed, Joyce and Kate volunteered to give Coleen an evening tour of the town while Shannon acquainted herself with the shop and the manager.

A few minutes after they left, a woman knocked on the front door. Shannon recognized her as the young woman she'd seen seated behind the counter, reading a book, the day they arrived.

Morgan Lombardi.

Shannon guessed the manager to be in her early thirties. She wore scruffy jeans and an electric blue blouse. Her medium-length black hair was pulled back into a loose ponytail. Her dark brown eyes were surrounded by black eyeliner—too much, in Shannon's opinion.

Shannon unlocked the deadbolt and opened the door, triggering the tinkle of the bell.

"Is it OK to come in now?" the woman asked.

"As far as I know. You must be Morgan?"

"I am." The manager strode in. "And you must be Victoria's granddaughter?"

"That's right."

They shook hands.

"Betty asked me to leave right before the meeting and return in an hour, per Victoria's wishes," Morgan said. "We don't usually close that early, although, it's past closing time now. Since you're going to be the new owner and all, I hope that was all right with you."

"Yes, of course."

Morgan locked the door and walked behind the counter, depositing her purse underneath. "I have a class coming in at one tomorrow. I thought I'd do a little prep work before calling it a day."

Two women appeared at the front entrance and tried to enter. Morgan pretended not to notice, so Shannon poked her head out the door and greeted them. "I'm sorry, but we're closed. I hope you'll come back again during our normal business hours."

The women mumbled apologies and headed off down the street.

Morgan leaned on the counter. "They never stop coming, especially during the tourist season. They want you to be open 24/7." She eyed Shannon. "You're pretty good with customers."

"I own an online craft business."

"That's cool." Morgan tapped a key on the register. The drawer popped open, and she began to count.

"Our meeting probably caused you to miss your evening bank deposit," Shannon commented.

Morgan shrugged. "It's no big deal. I stow the money in the safe if I can't get to the bank in time."

Shannon noticed some cash remained in the register when Morgan closed it again. "You leave money in the register overnight?"

"I always keep $100 or so in the change drawer."

"Shouldn't the day's earnings be deposited at the bank?"

Morgan scoffed. "No one's ever complained about how I do things."

Shannon blinked in disbelief, making a mental note to change that practice the moment she was officially given the keys to the place. "Would you mind showing me around?" she asked. "I'd like to get acquainted with the layout of the store."

Morgan unwrapped a piece of gum and shoved it into her mouth. "Why not? We can start at the loft area and work our way down."

As they climbed the stairs to the artist lofts Morgan explained the way things worked. Each "loft" was essentially an oversized cubicle with ten-foot walls and a door that locked; a few had windows. Some of the lofts were rented as work spaces, and others functioned as small shops. Artists leased the spaces on a monthly basis. The concept had proven to be successful; only two of the twelve spaces sat empty.

Down a second set of stairs, Morgan showed her the delivery and loading area, the offices, and the stockrooms. The office door still had her grandmother's name on it. A hand-painted sign in sage green, decorated with pink roses, featured her name in a charming Victorian-style font.

Shannon pushed open the door. The office was in need of a good cleaning, but other than that, it suited her. An eclectic mix of items lined its shelves. The desk held everything from samples to dolls to craft creations. Instead of a standard office lamp, a dainty, white wooden chandelier hung above the desk.

They continued on to the first stockroom. Shannon was disappointed to find the area in complete disarray. Shelves were stuffed to capacity with items, but there was no apparent rhyme or reason to their location. She glanced at Morgan who seemed oblivious, snapping and popping her gum.

The second stockroom looked much the same. Large tarp-covered lumps on the floor caught Shannon's attention. "What's that?"

Morgan reached for the doorknob, and tried to edge her back out. "It's nothing, just some equipment we're getting rid of. We have a buyer coming in tomorrow to take a look at it."

"Who do you mean by 'we'?" Shannon's eyes narrowed.

"You and I, the shop. You know."

"No, I don't know. I certainly haven't authorized the sale of any equipment."

Morgan lifted her chin in defiance. "Mrs. Paisley did."

Shannon suspected the woman was lying, or at the very least, withholding information. She lifted a corner of the tarp and then threw it off completely, revealing a curious assortment of equipment. "What's it for?"

"Your grandmother was interested in learning to silversmith jewelry, so she purchased some equipment and hired a man to come in and teach her."

Her interest piqued, Shannon asked, "Did she ever become a silversmith?"

"No," Morgan shook her head. "She took sick and never got around to it."

Shannon bent down to examine the equipment more closely. "This one looks like some kind of polisher." She pointed. "See the buffer cylinder?"

Morgan humored her with a slight smile.

Excited, Shannon ran her hand along another piece of equipment. "A kiln. I've never seen one this small. But I suppose for jewelry, you wouldn't need a large one." She stood up. "How fascinating."

"Well, don't get too used to this stuff. It'll probably be gone when the man leaves tomorrow."

"Excuse me?"

"The buyer. He's the silversmith who sold the equipment to Mrs. Paisley. He agreed to buy it back—at a discount, of course."

"Call him and tell him not to come. I'll get in touch with him later in the week."

Morgan stared back, a defiant look in her eyes. "But I was told to sell it."

Shannon moved forward and stood toe-to-toe with the woman. "As of tomorrow morning, I will be the new owner of this store. Nothing is to be sold or disposed of unless I say so. Do you understand?"

"She's going to be furious," Morgan muttered.

"She who?"

Morgan coughed. "The silversmith."

"I thought the silversmith was a man."

"He is. Did I say 'she'? I meant 'he'." *So Morgan is working with Barbara on the sly, and likely getting a cut of the proceeds.* Shannon fumed. The family seemed to have their eyes on everything that belonged to Victoria. "Have any other items been sold recently?"

"A few things."

"I want a list of everything sold off since my grandmother

passed away," Shannon ordered. "And furthermore, you and I are going to do an inventory of the entire store. Put it on the schedule for next week. In the meantime, I'll personally inventory the stockrooms."

"You're the boss." Morgan said. "But an inventory of this place is going to take a lot of time. There are thousands of small items to count. If you want it done fast, I'll have to call in the part-timers, and that'll cost you some money. How long do you plan on being here?"

Morgan's condescending tone drove Shannon to the brink of losing her temper. "Long enough. Call in the part-timers."

The woman folded her arms. "Seriously? Why go to so much trouble? We all know you're going to sell this place, take the money, and move back to whatever country you came from. We'll be left to hunt for jobs while you're rolling in cash."

"For your information, I'm not going anywhere." The decision that had been brewing in her heart since the day the attorney's letter arrived burst forth from her lips.

"You're staying on?"

Now that she'd said it, Shannon wished she'd picked a better time and a better person to share the news with. "That's right. And if you want to continue to work here, I suggest you conduct yourself in a more professional manner." She narrowed her eyes at the woman to show her she meant business.

Morgan protested, "I-I didn't realize there was any chance the store would stay open."

"There are two things I want from you immediately.

First, I want the buyer's phone number. I'll call him myself. And second, I want a list of every item that has been sold off or dispersed from this shop, outside of regular sales receipts, since my grandmother's death. I'll be in the office." She pointed to the doorway. "Please don't keep me waiting."

Morgan's mouth came unhinged.

As Shannon walked away, she called back over her shoulder, "Oh, and if *Barbara* is angry about any of this, tell her she can speak to me."

She ducked into the office and shut the door behind her. The manager was insufferable. How could her grandmother have kept her on? Unfortunately, she couldn't fire the woman on the spot. That would put her in a bad situation. She needed Morgan, at least for now. The transition would be difficult enough. Moving to Apple Grove. Getting used to life in America. Leaving friends and family behind. She needed someone at the store who could keep things running in the short term and bring her up to speed on how things were done and why.

Alec and Lara. She needed to talk to the twins. She hadn't even discussed her decision with them. But Coleen's words echoed through her mind. Her friend was right. Soon the children would forge lives for themselves, with spouses and children and jobs that would take them away from Wainscott, maybe even from Scotland.

She picked up her phone and dialed Lara's number.

Lara answered on the third ring, her voice groggy. "Hi, Mum."

"Hi, Darling. I'm sorry to wake you, but I have something very important I want to ask you and Alec."

"What is it?" Lara asked, instantly alert.

"How would you feel if I were to stay in America … indefinitely?"

"You mean you're thinking about *moving* there?"

"I am. Be honest, I want to know how you really feel about this." Shannon braced herself for the answer.

Much to her surprise, Lara let out a squeal of excitement. "This is incredible! Alec and I have already discussed it. We've been waiting to see what you'd do."

"You have?"

"Yes. We want you to be happy, and owning a craft store is the perfect fit for you. We'd love the chance to study abroad … we can afford it now, right?"

"I should think so," Shannon replied, taken aback by the unexpected turn the conversation had taken.

"Then it's settled. Alec and I will start the paperwork to study abroad at Portland University and plan to join you in Oregon for the next school year. Who knows, perhaps we'll decide to stay on 'indefinitely' too."

Tears of joy began to stream down Shannon's face. "Sweet daughter of mine, you have no idea how happy you've just made me."

"You deserve to be happy, Mum. Are you going to call Alec, or do I get to tell him?"

"You break the good news to him later, when he's awake. Tell him I will call him soon."

"Will do."

"Go back to sleep. Next time, I'll try and call you at a decent hour."

Lara yawned. "Sounds good."

"I love you."

"Love you too."

Shannon hung up and wiped the tears from her face. Her heart felt ten times lighter than it had when she'd stepped into the office. Knowing her kids would be with her as she started her new life in the United States meant more to her than anything.

A knock sounded on the door.

"Come in."

Morgan entered and handed Shannon a slip of paper. "Here's the name and number you asked for."

"Thank you. And the list?"

"I'm working on it, but I don't know if I can finish tonight before I need to leave. Can I get it to you tomorrow?"

"No later than tomorrow." Shannon picked up the office phone, but she noticed Morgan still lingered by the door. "Is there something else?"

"I wanted to apologize for my behavior earlier. I shouldn't have acted the way I did. You're the owner now—or you will be—and you deserve respect. I'm really happy to know you won't be selling the place after all."

"I appreciate that."

"Um, that's all I had to say. So, if I don't see you before I leave, have a good night." Morgan made a hasty exit.

Shannon watched her leave. Perhaps there was hope for the woman. If she had the presence of mind to apologize and set things right, it was possible the two of them might be able to work things out.

She held up the slip of paper Morgan had given her and punched in the number.

A man with a scratchy voice answered. "Hello?"

"Mr. Giddings? Harold Giddings?"

"That's me."

"My name is Shannon McClain. I'm Victoria Paisley's granddaughter."

He whistled. "I didn't know she had a granddaughter. I'm pleased to meet you."

"I was given your name by the manager of the craft store. She said you're interested in buying some of our equipment?"

"I sure am. I'll be there tomorrow."

Shannon cleared her throat. "I have a different proposition for you."

"What's that?"

"I understand my grandmother hired you to teach her silversmithing."

"That's correct. She bought the equipment from me, but she got sick before I could teach her how to use it."

"Well, what would you say about teaching me instead?"

"You?"

"I'm a beader. I create a lot of vintage looks. Necklaces, earrings, and bracelets. I would love to cast my own pendants and make silver rings, and more. Would you be willing to teach me the art? I'll hire you to do so, if you're interested."

"Well ..." He paused. "Can I meet you at the shop first? I like to size people up to see if they're cut out for this kind of work. Then I can show you the equipment and explain how the process works. If you still want to go forward after that, fine, you hire me and I'll teach you everything I know. But if you decide you don't want to mess with it, you promise to sell me the equipment back at the price Morgan offered."

Shannon took a deep breath. "We have a deal, Mr. Giddings. Would you be able to come Wednesday at 10 a.m.?"

"Make it Thursday and I'll be there."

"Thursday it is, Mr. Giddings."

Shannon hung up the phone and leaped from her chair. "Woo-hoo!" she yelled, feeling a wave of release as she did.

Silversmithing was something she'd always wanted to do. Beading was the first level, but learning to cast silver was the next—another lifelong dream coming true.

"Um, hello?" Coleen's voice drifted through the door. "Are you OK in there?"

Shannon chuckled. "Come in. I'm fine. I've had a very emotional evening and I needed to get some of it out of my system."

Coleen raised a brow. "I see. Do you think we should head back to the inn before you lose your marbles completely?"

"Ha, ha."

"Seriously, it's getting late, and you need to get a good night's sleep. Tomorrow's the big day."

The reading of the will.

"You're right. Let's go."

"I wonder if Barbara or any of her family will be there," Coleen mused.

"I don't know, but after everything that's happened, I'm not expecting a warm reception."

— 10 —

"No 'sleep crease' today, I see," Shannon tried to break the tension as she and Coleen climbed into their rental car the next morning. Shannon started the engine and they were soon on their way to the law office of Roger Barnwell.

"Thank goodness," Coleen replied. "I do have an unsightly bruise on my stomach, though."

"Perhaps you should refrain from sleeping with an oversized can of hair spray at your side."

Coleen scoffed. "After what happened the night before in the room near ours? Likely meant to *be* ours? No way am I sleeping unprotected."

Shannon laughed. "Of course, offering to fix a vandal's hair is a great way to get him to leave peacefully."

"Very funny. That was not my plan. If anyone so much as pokes a toe into our room, I intend to blind him with Ultra Hold so we can make a quick escape. If their hair happens to get fixed in the process they can thank me later."

Shannon shook her head. "What would I do without you?"

"Lead a dreadfully boring life." Coleen winked. "So, are you ready for this?"

"As ready as I'm going to be. At least after this meeting is over, the threats will stop. Once I legally take possession of the house and business, there's no point in anyone harassing me anymore."

"Or trying to kill you."

"*Coleen.*"

"I'm not saying someone was trying to kill you, but theoretically, if they did, after today, everything would go to Alec and Lara and whoever else you wanted it to. Not Barbara and her family."

"True." Shannon turned the corner and descended a steep hill, following the commands from the GPS. "I think I see the street we need to turn on up ahead."

Coleen checked her watch. "We're a little early. I wonder if—"

"Oh no!" Shannon stomped hard on the brake pedal. "I think there's something wrong with the brakes." She continued to pump the pedal frantically, as the car picked up speed on the downhill.

"Push harder!" Coleen urged. She pulled up on the emergency break between the seats, but the car continued to gain momentum.

"I'm stepping on it as hard as I can." Shannon looked ahead to the three-way intersection at the bottom of the hill. If she didn't stop, they'd run over the curb and straight into a brick building. "I've got to run this thing into the grass. Hold on!"

Shannon jerked the wheel to the right. The car bounced up over a low curb, crossed the sidewalk, and rolled to a bumpy stop in the grass.

"I cannot believe that just happened." Shannon stared in shock as smoke began to pour out from under the hood. "Are you all right?"

"No." Coleen gulped, brushing her hair off her face

with trembling fingers. "And I take back everything I just said. Someone is *definitely* trying to kill you."

* * *

Shannon burst through the front doors of the law office.

The receptionist looked up, a startled expression on her face. "May I help you?"

"I'm Shannon McClain. I have a ten-thirty appointment with Mr. Barnwell." Shannon fought to keep her voice steady; her emotions were still running high from the accident.

The receptionist checked her computer. "He's already in the conference room, I'm not sure—"

"Never mind. I'll show myself in." Shannon breezed past the desk and headed for the two double doors marked 'conference,' ignoring the receptionist's protests.

She flung open the doors with so much force that they slammed into the walls. "I'm here. Do not start without me."

The three people seated at the end of a long conference table looked up with a start.

"Shannon?" asked the man at the head of the table, adjusting his tie.

"That's me. Sorry I'm late. I was in an accident on the way here. I had to walk the rest of the way." She glared at the older couple seated at the table. *Barbara and Trevor, thinking me dead, no doubt.*

"I hope it wasn't serious?" Mr. Barnwell asked.

"It could have been." She continued to focus her accusing gaze on the couple. "Brake failure. But fortunately, I survived. My friend stayed with the car to wait for the police and make arrangements to have it towed."

"I'm glad you weren't hurt. I'm Roger Barnwell. Please, have a seat. We were just about to get started. Your timing is perfect."

She took a seat on the attorney's left, directly across from the couple, and the old woman narrowed her eyes at Shannon.

Mr. Barnwell slid his eyeglasses down the bridge of his nose. "This is Barbara Kilgore, Victoria's sister, and her husband, Trevor. I presume you haven't met before today?"

"No," Shannon said. "And I hope I never see them again."

Trevor slammed a fist on the table. "You ungrateful brat!"

"Trevor." Barbara placed a restraining hand on his arm. "Calm down."

Mr. Barnwell cleared his throat. "Mr. Kilgore, I'm going to have to ask you both to leave. The will no longer concerns you now that Mrs. McClain has arrived."

Trevor pushed himself to his feet. He pointed an accusatory finger at Shannon. "This should be mine. You owe me."

"I don't owe you a thing," Shannon hissed. "You've done nothing but harass me since the day Victoria died."

"If it weren't for me, you'd have been dead a long time ago."

Barbara stood and pulled her husband toward the door. "Not here, Trevor."

Shannon stood. "No, if it *were* up to you, I'd be dead. Tampering with my brakes isn't the most subtle way to get rid of me. Neither is leaving threatening notes on my door, trying to steal my passport, or ransacking hotel rooms."

"I don't know what you're trying to imply," the old man sputtered. "Frankly, I don't care. You're nothing but a selfish kid, just like your mother."

Shannon felt tears sting her eyes. "You know nothing about me."

"That's *enough*," Barbara finally succeeded in pulling the old man from the room, casting one last venomous look over her shoulder at Shannon.

That's when Shannon noticed the other person in the room. Michael Stone, dressed in a tailored black suit, leaned against the back wall near the door. His arms were folded across his broad chest; his expression was murderous.

"What are *you* doing here?" she demanded.

"I'll answer that," Mr. Barnwell replied, appearing a little flustered. "But first, why don't we all sit back down?"

Shannon lowered herself into her chair while Michael chose the seat directly across from her. Their gazes locked, and his blue eyes held hers with no sign of letting go.

"Mr. Stone is here because your grandmother hired him to be here," Mr. Barnwell said.

Shannon looked away first, breaking the spell. "Why would she do that?"

"Mr. Stone owns a security firm. Most of his dealings are with corporations, but he does work for private customers as well. Your grandmother wanted to be certain of your safety during the transition process."

"She expected someone would try to prevent me from claiming my inheritance," Shannon speculated.

"It's not uncommon. I see this sort of thing happen all too often with inheritances. Victoria was concerned certain relatives might give you trouble about the will. So she hired Mr. Stone in advance."

Shannon shook her head, trying to process it all. Then she turned to Michael. "Fine job you're doing, protecting me. You're a bit late."

Michael's jaw clenched. "You should've told me about the threats the other night at the inn when I asked what you knew about the break-in."

How dare he be angry with me. "Perhaps instead of poking fun at my accent, you should've told me who you were."

"Time out." Mr. Barnwell held up his hands in a *T*. "We've got a lot to get through here and I have another meeting in an hour. Can you save this conversation for later so we can proceed with the reading of the will?"

"Of course." Shannon turned her attention to the attorney. "Let's get on with this, please."

Mr. Barnwell shuffled the papers in front of him and began to read. Shannon listened to each page he read, trying to ignore the unsettling feeling caused by Michael's close proximity.

The attorney read the will in its entirety, a tedious tome of paperwork. Eventually, when Shannon found it impossible to keep her focus any longer, she stood and made a quick trip to the coffee pot on a side table. Though coffee was not her beverage of choice, Shannon sucked down two cups before Mr. Barnwell finally concluded.

"Do you understand, Mrs. McClain?" he asked.

"Yes, I believe so, but could you clarify something for

me? According to what you've read, I'm to receive a large estate, including fifteen acres of property that will require extensive upkeep, and a business experiencing financial difficulties. However, I did not hear you mention any savings or cash. Is this correct?"

Mr. Barnwell hesitated for a moment before answering. "That's correct. There is a modest sum of cash for you to use to pay this year's taxes and carry on for a short while, but after that, you'll be on your own as far as maintaining the estate and the business."

"From what I understand, certain family members were a drain on Victoria's finances. Is that why there's no cash reserve in the estate?"

Mr. Barnwell cleared his throat. "I'd rather not speculate."

"I understand." Shannon sat back in her chair, her mind wandering to Barbara and her deplorable husband.

"Very well, then." Mr. Barnwell opened a large envelope. "Here are the keys to the mansion and the summer house."

"Thank you."

He pulled out another cluster of keys. "These go to the business."

Shannon took them from him.

"And the keys to the vehicle are somewhere in the garage, as I understand it."

"There's a vehicle? I must have missed that."

"Yes, an old pickup truck."

"That should be interesting. I've never driven a truck before."

Mr. Barnwell shuffled his pile of papers around. "It's a 1955 Ford."

"Does it still run?"

"I don't know."

Michael broke his stony silence. "When I take you to the estate, I'll look it over and see if we can get it to start. If not, there's a garage on the edge of town that does good work at reasonable prices."

Shannon stared at him, mouth agape. "When *you* take me to the estate?"

"You'd prefer to drive yourself there in a car with no brakes?" he countered.

Shannon pursed her lips, considering his words.

His expression softened. "I'd like to do the job Victoria hired me to do. It would make matters a good deal easier if you'd allow me to."

"That was Victoria's wish," Mr. Barnwell added. "For Mr. Stone to ensure a safe transition."

Shannon sighed. "Fine. You can drive me to the estate. But first we need to find Coleen and settle the issue with the rental car. And I'd also like to stop by the store."

"There is one last thing," Mr. Barnwell said. "Michael, would you mind stepping out for a moment?"

Michael nodded and left the room.

Mr. Barnwell pulled out a white envelope from a manila folder and handed it to her.

"What's this?" she asked.

"A private letter to you from your grandmother. She instructed I give it to you upon the conclusion of our meeting. You can read it at your leisure, but as per her wishes, this letter is for your eyes only."

"Thank you." Her fingers itched to rip it open on the

spot. She stood to leave, impatient to find a place where she could devour its contents in private.

"She wanted me to warn you ..."

"Yes?"

"For your own safety, destroy it when you're through reading it."

— 11 —

Michael's car turned down the drive to the house, which sat back about a quarter of a mile from the main road. Shannon noticed nary an inch of ground close to the turn-off wasn't covered by either trees or creeping ivy and a dazzling array of wildflowers.

The house itself sat in a clearing at a higher elevation. As the car climbed, Shannon thought she caught a glimpse of a body of water a short distance away.

How did I miss that before?

Surrounded by such beauty, she felt her irritation at her store manager lessen. Morgan still hadn't completed the list she'd requested, making their stop at the craft store a wasted effort.

Michael glanced back at Shannon. She was aware of his glance, but she kept her head pressed to the passenger window in the back-seat, staring at the impressive landscape surrounding them.

"I wonder how old the mansion is," Coleen said. "Didn't Betty say Victoria had lived here for a long time?"

"As I understand it, the home was built in the 1930s by Shannon's great-grandparents," Michael said.

They pulled to a stop in the circle drive, got out of the car, and walked to the front door.

Filled with anticipation, Shannon rifled through the

keys, searching for the right key to the door. *My new home.*

Michael noticed what she was doing. "I don't think we'll need that. Nobody locks their doors around here."

But as he turned the knob and tried to push the door open, he nearly planted his face in the door, for the deadbolt was locked.

"That's strange," he muttered.

Shannon suppressed a victorious smile and found the key, appropriately labeled.

"Allow me." She edged him out of the way and unlocked the door. Then she opened it herself.

"She's a stubborn one," Coleen stage-whispered to Michael.

In the foyer stood a large circular table crafted from solid marble with black inlays in a Grecian wave design. In the middle of it, a crystal vase overflowed with a delightful bouquet of spring blooms.

Shannon turned her focus to the imposing statue next to the grand staircase. It was a Roman soldier on a black stallion that was rearing up at the sight of a venomous snake on the ground below. She ran her hand along the cool black marble.

Coleen joined her. "My goodness, that statue is twice as tall as you. How does anyone dust it properly?"

Shannon noticed another statue, of a woman holding a vase on her shoulder, farther down a hall off the foyer. Insets in the wall spotlighted two Greco-Roman busts. Fascinated, she made up her mind to explore all of the nooks and crannies of the mansion when she had time alone. She hoped to find more examples of amazing art.

A strong wind caught the open door, slamming it shut behind Coleen.

"Och!" she gasped.

At the sound, Deborah emerged from somewhere in the back of the house, a leery look on her face until she recognized them.

"I thought I heard a commotion." The woman wiped her hands on a white kitchen apron and approached Shannon. "It's good to see you again. Welcome to the Paisley Manor."

"Thank you."

The housekeeper opened her arms to Michael. "And you, I'm waiting for my hug."

He smiled and embraced the woman. When they drew apart, she squinted at him. "How is it you get more handsome every time I see you?"

"I suspect it's because your eyesight gets a little worse every time you see me."

Deborah laughed and turned to Shannon. "I imagine you're anxious to have a look at what your old grandmama left you. Let me show you around the place."

She led the women toward the first set of doors to the right of the main entryway.

Instead of following them, Michael moved toward the front door. "I have to meet with a client, but I shouldn't be gone long." He glanced at Shannon. "When I get back, we can take a look at the truck."

"Take your time," Deborah replied. "I have a lot to show them."

She slid open the pocket-door panels to reveal a large room decorated with a mixture of antique and classic traditional furniture. Murals on two of the walls depicted scenes of the sea.

"This is the drawing room," Deborah said.

"How beautiful." Shannon drew closer to a mural for a better look. "Victoria must have loved the water."

"She did, but she loved a man of the sea more. Her late husband, James, was a ship's captain."

"Did Victoria paint these?"

"No. Your mother painted them."

"Really?" She'd longed to hear more about her mother. To find out they had something in common—an artistic bent—made her heart sing. "They're amazing."

"She was a talented artist. With many different media, mind you. And she was a wonderful photographer as well."

Coleen moved closer. Her reading glasses perched atop the bridge of her nose, she examined the murals.

"Such talent." Coleen pointed at Shannon. "This must be where my friend gets it. She can master any craft she sets her mind to. Beading, needlepoint, knitting, crochet ... and I believe she's done some painting as well."

Embarrassed, Shannon tried to shush her. "Just a touch."

"You should see her work," Coleen insisted.

Deborah brought her hands together. "I'd love to. I'm a quilter, you know. Victoria and I used to quilt together over the winter when the weather turned bad. Plus, James used to be away for months at a time. She and I had plenty of time to quilt then, or to craft as she pleased. That's how the Paisley Craft Market & Artist Lofts came to be."

"What happened to my grandfather?"

"His ship was lost at sea. They never found his body. There's a painting of him in the hallway leading to Victoria's old room. I'll be sure to point it out to you when we tour the upstairs rooms."

Following Deborah through the grand mansion, Shannon became so engrossed in the tour that she put off her desire to be alone so she could read Victoria's letter.

Deborah stepped inside another room. "And this is the dining room."

Similar pocket doors separated it from the entryway. The room was painted a delicate cream and was trimmed with white crown molding. Exotic items from across the globe adorned the walls.

A long table, made of teakwood and topped with two bronze candelabras, dominated the room. Side tables were set with tureens and fresh floral arrangements. A bronze chandelier cast with floral designs and cherubs hung overhead, laden with faceted crystals.

The table was set for twelve with fine bone china and elegant silverware.

Coleen picked up a glass to inspect it. She pinged the stemware with her finger, admiring the resulting tone. "These are high quality."

"Of course," Deborah said. "Victoria worked hard all her life, and she had a discerning nature. Only the best would do. Not that she was materialistic, mind you. I don't want you to get the wrong impression. She gave generously too."

"She sounds like a very interesting woman. I wish I could've known her while she was alive," Shannon said.

"Would you like to see the study?"

A smaller room next to the drawing room proved to be the study. But instead of typical masculine décor, the room was light and airy, filled with feminine fabrics of pink, lavender, and light green. A large worktable set near the window served as a desk, and it was filled with various craft projects.

An easel in the corner, partially covered by a cloth, revealed a landscape in progress. Craft books lined maple shelves along one entire wall.

"How delightful." Coleen pointed at the chandelier. Decorated with vintage teacups, it hung in the center of the room.

Two overstuffed chairs and a low coffee table filled another corner of the study. Shannon admired pots of pink *Phalaenopsis* orchids scattered along the windowsill in full bloom.

"I love this room," Shannon said. "I could see myself spending a lot of time in here."

"This used to be James's stuffy old study until Victoria took it over. Out of all the rooms in the house, it's my favorite as well."

Shannon's phone buzzed in her pocket.

"We'll wait for you in the kitchen," Deborah said, leaving Shannon alone in the study.

"Hello." There was no reply. "Hello?"

"Oh, Shannon?" a woman asked.

"Speaking. Who is this?"

"It's Nadine, dear. I didn't expect you to answer ... so fast. How are you?"

"It's been a bit of a rough morning, but I'm fine now. Are you calling about dinner?" Shannon sank into a nearby chair.

"Yes. I'm really looking forward to it. But I wondered, could we make it a late lunch instead? I'm already in town, visiting with an old friend. I could meet you at, say, two o'clock?"

"Two o'clock it is. Why don't you come to Victoria's house? We can decide where to go from here."

Nadine was silent for a moment. "I thought you were staying at the inn?"

"I was. But I plan to move into the house today. I've decided to remain in Apple Grove for … a while."

"Why, that's marvelous, darling. That means we'll have lots of time to get to know one another. I'll see you this afternoon."

Shannon hung up and suddenly remembered Victoria's letter. She was finally alone, but for how long? She decided not to risk being interrupted while reading it. She could wait a little longer.

She cut through an impressive butler's pantry and joined Deborah and Coleen in the kitchen. As she entered the room, she felt her jaw drop.

Coleen laughed at her expression. "Can you believe the size of this kitchen? You could fit twelve cooks in here."

The tops of the counters and center island were made of rose granite. Above the large island hung copper pots and pans, all polished to perfection. A delicate vase on the windowsill, laden with larkspur and bright yellow chrysanthemums, caught her eye.

"Look at this," Coleen said. "Double ovens in stainless steel, a professional cooktop, and warming drawers. Why, you could open your own restaurant."

Shannon chuckled. "No, thanks. I've got enough on my plate as it is." She examined the backsplash set with tiny iridescent tiles that mimicked waves and sea billows. At intervals, mosaic fish leaped from the water in splendid form. "Even the backsplash is a masterpiece."

"Takes your breath away, doesn't it?" Deborah ran her hand along one of the counters. "You should have seen it before the renovation. Oh, and there's a breakfast room to your right."

Coleen brought her hands to her face. "I've never seen anything so fine. I'm speechless."

Shannon raised a brow. "Speechless? You?"

"Ha ha."

Deborah continued. "All new top-of-the-line appliances, including the refrigerator."

Shannon spun around. "Where is the refrigerator?"

Deborah grinned and pointed to a wall of cabinets. "Blends right in with the cabinetry, doesn't it?"

"Clever." Shannon thought for a moment. "May I ask you a question?"

"Of course."

"You mentioned everything was new. Since my grandmother was so ill, why did she do such a huge renovation of the kitchen?"

Deborah corrected her. "Not only the kitchen, but the entire house. Including the summer house."

"But I was under the impression she was confined to her room most of the time during her last days."

"She was. She did it for you. In the event you decided to stay and live here, she wanted you to have a 'new' home to move into. She feared there wouldn't be much in the way of disposable assets to fund proper renovations. In the event you chose to sell it, she knew that remodeled kitchens and bathrooms would be key assets in attracting buyers."

Shannon was overcome with emotion. "It's still hard to fathom, that this woman I never knew would do all of this for me."

"I can imagine." Deborah regarded her fondly. "Shall we continue on? There's a lot more for you to see."

— 12 —

Michael lifted the brass knocker and let it fall three times. Less than a minute later, the door creaked open.

"Ah, Mr. Stone. Please come in."

He entered the dim foyer and surveyed his surroundings.

The elderly gentleman bid him to follow. "This way, please. Mr. Wallace is in the library."

The servant showed him into a library, its burgeoning shelves filled with hardcover books from floor to ceiling. Instead of a desk, two dark leather chairs were set at an angle with a tall table between them.

The client, an elderly man, sat in one of the chairs. He was dressed in blue and white striped pajamas with a matching silk robe belted around the waist. A gray Persian cat purred on his lap.

"Mr. Stone. Thank you for coming. May I commend you for being on time? So many people take the element of promptness lightly these days."

"Time is money, Mr. Wallace."

"Please have a seat. I hope you'll excuse my attire. I haven't been well."

Michael sat in the other chair. "I'm sorry to hear that."

"Would you care for something to drink? I can ring for whatever you'd like."

"No, thank you. I'm fine."

The man brought his fingertips together and tapped them. "Well then, perhaps we should proceed straight to the matter. I'm sure you're wondering why I requested this last-minute meeting."

Michael waited for the man to continue, his face impassive.

"I represent a client who would like you to follow and observe someone," Mr. Wallace said.

"For what purpose?"

"My client feels this individual might lead them to a certain item they are looking for."

Michael regarded him warily. "What sort of item?"

"A necklace."

"Is it stolen?"

"Not exactly."

Michael leaned forward in his chair, hands clasped. "I'm going to require a lot more information than that before I can make a decision about whether or not to take the job."

The old man grimaced. "The item belonged to a recently deceased relation. My client feels this item should rightfully belong to them as opposed to the individual who was bequeathed the estate."

"And is the individual in question in possession of this necklace?"

The man coughed. "Not exactly."

"Again, Mr. Wallace, cryptic answers will not suffice."

The old man scratched the cat's ears, considering his words. "It is believed to be hidden somewhere on the estate."

"What's the value of the necklace?"

The man locked rheumy eyes on him. "The value is estimated to be over $350,000."

"No wonder they're anxious to retrieve the piece." Even as he said the words, Michael began to put two and two together. "Are you speaking about the estate of Victoria Paisley?"

The man stared back. "How astute you are."

"Then I assume the individual you want me to follow and observe is her granddaughter, Shannon, the principal heir of the estate?"

"Yes. And my client is prepared to make it very much worth your while if you recover the necklace."

"Is that right?" Michael sat back in the chair. "Tell me more."

* * *

"Would you like to see the summer house?" Deborah opened the back door off the kitchen to reveal a fern-lined pathway leading to a sparkling blue lake.

Shannon followed the woman down the stone pathway with Coleen close behind. Beyond asparagus ferns lining the path, the area was thick with blooming flowers: poppies, hyacinths, larkspurs, zinnias and lilacs—all exuding a kaleidoscope of color and fragrance.

Shannon turned to her friend. "Pinch me. This is too good to be true."

"I'm overwhelmed. I can only imagine how you must feel."

The path branched off in two directions. One led directly to the lake and a wooden dock. The other led to the summer house.

The summer house, also of Mediterranean design, was

a one-story structure, a miniature version of the big house.

Shannon inhaled deeply. With rose trellises on both sides, the walk to the summer house's front porch was a fragrant one. Ornamental white wisteria and wedding wreath bushes, abundant lilies, and ferns lined the way.

As they entered through the arched doorway, she noticed a carving in the wood of the door.

"*Mìle fàilte*," she read aloud. "Was my grandmother Scottish?"

"Yes," Deborah answered. "Didn't you know?"

Shannon ran her fingers over the inscription. "No."

"'A thousand welcomes,'" Coleen translated the Gaelic phrase. "What a perfect greeting for a front door."

Shannon noticed a bronze bell above the door, with a metal chain hanging down from it. "What's this?"

"The doorbell," Deborah explained. "Victoria preferred to keep things simple in the cottage, more rustic. No electric doorbell."

Coleen raised her brows. "No heat or air conditioning either?"

"No, but there are lights. And a ceiling fan."

The cottage boasted a stone fireplace and one cozy bathroom. A blue-and-white gingham loveseat and two matching overstuffed chairs took up most of the available space in the main room. An old trunk between them served as a coffee table.

"My grandmother certainly loved books," Shannon remarked, eyeing the large bookshelf lining one entire wall.

The side of the house facing the lake was nothing but glass—windows that could be opened to the water, fitted with mesh screens to winnow bugs from the pleasant breeze. As she looked out the window, a cool wind lifted her hair. Bamboo and reeds grew along the water's edge. Lily pads floated on the surface.

"Charming, isn't it?" Deborah asked. "Victoria spent a lot of time out here. She loved to be close to nature."

Shannon turned to Deborah. "I can see why. Too bad there's no bed; one could easily stay all night."

"There *is* a bed." The woman turned and gestured toward a large bookshelf. "It's a Murphy bed." She gripped a latch near the wood trim and tugged. The shelf swung open like a door and a full-sized bed fell slowly from the wall behind it.

"Clever."

"Your grandmother was clever indeed. There's more ground to cover, unless you'd like a break?"

"No." Shannon straightened. "Show me all of it."

Back in the main house, Deborah took Shannon on a short tour of the rooms on the second and third floors.

"This was Victoria's room." Deborah entered the room ahead of Shannon to open curtains and windows. The open drapery revealed a sun-washed balcony. Shannon stepped out onto it and a partial view of the ocean greeted her.

"She loved the view and the breeze." Deborah said. "She used to stand on the balcony every morning and say her prayers."

Shannon leaned on the railing and closed her eyes for a moment, trying to imagine her grandmother doing the same.

"As Victoria instructed, I've cleaned out all of her clothes and personal belongings from the room. Should you decide to move in, it's ready for you. The only items she requested that I leave for you were family pictures and her Bible. You'll find the Bible in the nightstand drawer."

"Thank you." Shannon stepped back inside the room. "I'm glad you brought that up. I've decided I'd like to move in tonight."

"Must we leave Betty and the inn so soon?" Coleen protested. "I'm really going to miss the delicious breakfast."

"My sister's cooking is good, but mine is better," Deborah said with a wink.

The afternoon sun streamed through the floor-to-ceiling windows, curtains billowing like sails in the soft breeze. The four-poster bed of carved teak was canopied with crocheted lace draping the top and front. The two sides were drawn, but they could be released to completely enclose the bed. Colorful silk pillows embroidered with flowers and exotic birds decorated the bed.

As Shannon took it all in, her gaze landed on a wall filled with photographs. She gasped. "*What* is this?"

Coleen hurried to the wall for a closer look. "They're all pictures of you!"

Four rows of pictures. She'd passed right by them on the way in. She counted the photos, one for every year of her life until the age of thirty-five.

"Victoria took great delight in watching you grow up," Deborah said.

Shannon traced her index finger along the photographic timeline of her life. Mounted in identical glossy black frames, the pictures brought back painful memories. The picture of her at the age of four revealed the pain of losing her mother. The years that followed showed a progression of grief, sorrow, anger, frustration, and, finally, resolve.

"How did she come by all these pictures of me?"

"Your father."

Shannon's mind reeled at the revelation. "I don't understand. He would never even talk to me about my mother or her family."

Deborah's expression was pained. "I'm sorry. I wish I could give you answers."

Shannon pounded her fist on the wall, rattling the frames. "If Victoria cared about me so much, why didn't she ever try to contact me? None of this makes any sense."

Coleen patted her shoulder. "We'll figure it out. Don't despair. Perhaps your Great-Aunt Nadine can help."

Shannon took a deep breath. "I hope so. I'm having lunch with her later today."

Deborah said nothing. She walked to the balcony window, closed the French doors, and drew the drapes. "I could use a cup of tea before lunch. How about you girls?"

"I'd love one," Coleen replied.

An idea came to Shannon. "That would be wonderful, thank you Deborah. But could I ask of favor of you girls?"

Deborah and Coleen exchanged glances.

"My Aunt Nadine and I are meeting here. We were going to drive into town for lunch, but it would be much more convenient if …"

"Say no more." Deborah put her arm around Coleen. "I'll take care of your friend. We'll visit Gertrude at the tearoom. I'll have her whip up something special."

"Is that all right with you, Coleen?" Shannon asked.

"Of course it is. I might be able to sneak in some shopping while we're at it."

Deborah scrubbed her hands together. "Now that we've settled that matter, let's get to the kitchen."

A short while later they all sat around the table in the breakfast room in comfortable silence, each sipping their tea.

"I'm surprised Michael hasn't returned yet," Deborah commented.

"Speaking of Michael," Coleen began, ignoring Shannon's pained look. "What's *his* story?"

"His 'story'?"

"Yeah, you know, is he single?"

Shannon tried to kick Coleen under the table. Her foot collided instead with a table leg. "Och."

Confused, Deborah looked at her, then back to Coleen. "Yes, he's single. His wife, Angela, was killed many years ago by a member of a drug cartel that Michael infiltrated during his time as a police detective in Portland. A 'revenge killing,' I believe it was called."

"Oh, how awful," Shannon said.

"It was. The guilt nearly destroyed him."

"Does he have any children?" Coleen asked.

"No."

"You said his wife died many years ago. Do you know if he's dating anyone now?" Coleen pressed.

"Coleen, please." Shannon shook her head.

Coleen's eyes widened innocently. "What? I'm just making conversation."

"As far as I know, he hasn't been in a serious relationship with a woman since his wife died," Deborah said. "I think he feels like it was his fault she was killed."

Shannon recalled how angry he'd been at her earlier in the day after hearing about the threats she'd received. *Now it makes sense. He feels like he's failing to protect me—a job he promised Victoria he'd do.*

"Hello?" a deep voice called out. "Anybody home?"

"In the breakfast room, Michael," Deborah answered.

Michael's muscular form filled the doorway. He'd removed his suit jacket and rolled up the sleeves of his gray button-down shirt to his elbows.

He nodded to Shannon. "I apologize for making you wait. My meeting took longer than I'd anticipated."

"Tough client?" asked Deborah.

"Interesting client. Now, shall we go take a look at the truck?"

— 13 —

Joined by Coleen and Deborah, Shannon followed Michael to a detached garage on the side of the house. Covered in old dead vines, its paint was peeling, and its windows were coated with dust and dirt. Though her grandmother had put forth a concentrated effort to renovate and update the rest of the house, it was apparent the old garage had not received any attention for a number of years.

Michael went in through a side entrance and hit the button on the door opener. The door squeaked and popped as it slid to the ceiling, revealing an old truck in the center of the garage.

Coleen blinked. "That's the most hideous thing I've ever seen."

Shannon walked around it, inspecting it from all sides. "The attorney did fail to mention the color. I've never seen a blue so ..."

"Blinding?" Coleen wrinkled her nose. "Did he leave out the part about the big rust spots too?"

"The truck's a classic," Michael said, lifting the hood to poke around the engine. "It just needs a little TLC."

"What's that?" Shannon asked.

Deborah folded her arms. "Tender loving care. And forget about TLC. What this truck needs is a miracle."

"Do you have the keys?" Michael asked.

Deborah glanced behind him. "There's a hook on the back wall. You can't miss them. The key fob's the same color as the truck."

He found them right away, jangling them in his hand as he walked to the cab. He swung open the heavy door with a loud squeak. "They don't make them like this anymore."

"I can't imagine why," Coleen muttered.

With a loud clanging and a couple of gasps, the truck started up, releasing a noxious cloud of fumes into the garage. The women parted as he threw the truck into gear and pulled out into the drive beside the house.

"It's like a spy car—comes with its own smokescreen," Coleen coughed. "I can't imagine riding around in that horrid truck."

Shannon laughed. "Oh, come on. It'll be fun driving around in a 'classic' automobile. Think of it as an adventure."

"We'll need gas masks just to survive a trip around the corner."

Still coughing, Coleen and Deborah retreated to a porch on the side of the house. But Shannon stayed with the truck.

Left arm resting on the rolled-down window, Michael said, "I'm going to take her for a spin, see how she runs. Care to join me?"

Shannon motioned to the other women, but they adamantly shook their heads and remained on the porch.

"I guess this is as good a time as any to start getting used to it." Wishing she had a stepladder, Shannon climbed up into the passenger's seat.

The dashboard was cracked in two places. The long bench seat, sans center divider, was done in cream and aqua leather with three upholstery buttons at intervals. The steering wheel was thin and black and stuck up high from the dashboard.

Shannon was surprised by the spaciousness of the cab. Most modern cars were small and cramped by comparison.

"Do you know a lot about old cars and trucks?" she asked.

But Michael didn't respond, and she soon figured out why. With the windows down, the noise of the engine drowned out any possibility of normal conversation.

He took them for a short drive down the coastal highway. She leaned her head against the frame and closed her eyes, allowing the wind to whip her hair. The clouds that had blotted out the sun earlier in the day were gone, and golden warmth soaked her skin.

The two shared an occasional glance, but neither attempted to speak. Surprisingly, she felt the absence of conversation didn't create an uncomfortable void between them. In fact, the opposite was true. Their shared silence was comfortable. It was an odd thing, how sitting next to a man she hardly knew could feel so comforting.

Don't overthink it. It's been a trying day.

Though the truck sputtered and clanged as if on its last leg, Michael didn't seem concerned. When he turned it around to head back, Shannon felt her spirits wilt. She would've been content to continue on their trek for hours. With the passenger side now facing the water, she watched the glimmer and sparkle of blue waves crashing onto the shore as the tide began to shift and change.

By the end of the drive, she guessed they'd traveled about three kilometers or so.

Back at the mansion, after poking around under the hood again, Michael pronounced the truck "drivable." He then excused himself to go back to work, leaving the women alone.

Shannon looked at her watch. "Nadine will be here soon."

She hurried inside to freshen up, choosing to save Victoria's letter for the evening, when she could curl up, relax, and focus on her grandmother's first and last words to her.

* * *

Nadine rang the bell at two o'clock sharp. She pulled Shannon into a warm embrace the moment she opened the door.

"Darling, thank you for making time in your busy schedule to visit with your old aunt." She kissed Shannon on the cheek.

"No need to thank me. I'm so glad you came."

"Where would you like to have lunch? I'll drive. My car's ready to go." She waved a perfectly manicured hand at the sleek Cadillac parked in the drive.

Shannon looked at her aunt's lemon-colored linen pant suit and tried to picture her rambling down the road in the old blue truck. A slight chuckle escaped her lips at the thought. "Actually, I thought we could stay here, if that's OK. Deborah's whipped up something special for us."

Nadine's face lit up. "I'd love that. Deborah is a fabulous cook. Is she in?"

Shannon ushered Nadine inside. "No, she and Coleen have made themselves scarce for the rest of the afternoon. They've gone shopping in town."

Nadine breezed through the foyer, slowing down to peer into the drawing room as she passed.

"I've always loved that old clock. Does it still work?"

Shannon eyed the elaborate timepiece on the mantle. Cast in bronze, with cherubs on either side, the clock face was fashioned out of ivory with gold settings. "It appears to be working."

"That clock holds so many memories," Nadine mused. "We grew up with it. Papa gave it to my sister before he died. I remember how he used to wind it every evening by the light of the fire. Then he'd tell us stories before we went to bed." She sighed. "How I adore it."

"It is lovely," Shannon agreed.

"Forgive me. I get nostalgic whenever I come here. Victoria was so good about keeping pieces like that from the past."

"No need to apologize. I understand. Are you hungry?"

Nadine hooked her arm through Shannon's. "I am. Something smells delicious."

Once seated at the table, they enjoyed light conversation over Deborah's specialty, pesto chicken stew with cheese dumplings.

"You're so beautiful. And you look a lot like Beth," Nadine brooded. "I'm just sick that we've lost all of these years with you."

"So am I." Shannon worked up her courage. "About my

mother, I was wondering, do you know anything about her disappearance?"

Nadine lowered her eyes to her bowl. "I know a few facts. What have you been told?"

"Nothing, really. I've learned since my arrival that she was a very artistic woman. And I believe she was a journalist, or studying to be one. But that's it."

"I see." Nadine set down her spoon. "Then I will tell you the sad truth about your mother. But I warn you, it will be difficult to hear."

Shannon felt her heart skip a beat. "I don't care. I want to know the truth."

"Your mother was very ill."

"Was it cancer?"

"No, not a physical illness. Mental."

"Oh." The news struck Shannon like a blow to the gut. "How so?"

"The doctors believed she had a multiple personality disorder. When she left you and your father, she wasn't leaving as the woman you knew. She'd slipped back into an alternate personality."

Shannon's mind raced. "That is … unbelievable."

"I know. And I'm so sorry I have to be the one to tell you."

"What happened to her after she left Scotland?" Shannon pressed.

"She arrived here, clearly out of her mind. Victoria paid for her to go to a treatment center to get help."

"You mean she put her in a mental hospital?"

"You don't mince words, do you, dear?" Nadine chuckled,

and then her expression grew cold. "But you're right. She hid Beth away in an institution. Less chance she would embarrass the family that way. Victoria was always concerned with appearances."

"Where is she now?"

Nadine paused. Tears formed in the corners of her eyes and she dabbed them away with her napkin. "She's been dead for over thirty years. Beth died in that institution, alone. And so did the dark secret of the family."

Shannon felt a tear slide down her cheek, and she hurried to wipe it off. "But how did she die? Weren't they monitored?"

"I don't know all of the details. Victoria swept the incident under the rug as best she could. From what I understand, another patient flew into a fit of rage and attacked Beth. By the time the orderlies got to her, it was too late. Such a tragic situation. Your mother was simply in the wrong place at the wrong time."

Shannon felt her stomach turn. She pushed her food away. "I can't believe this. It's more horrific than anything I'd imagined."

"Darling," Nadine reached across the table and took her hand. "I know you're considering a move here, but this mansion is full of nothing but heartache and secrets. I urge you to leave. Go home to your life in Scotland. Forget about this place."

Shannon kept her gaze on their clasped hands as she considered her great-aunt's words.

"I can help you sell the house and the business," Nadine continued. "There's no need for you to even be here. Inventory the items in the house before you go, and I'll see that they're sold for top dollar. It's the least I can do for you."

Shannon shook her head. "As awful as all of this is, I truly feel like I'm supposed to remain here, in Apple Grove."

Nadine pulled her hand away, sighing. "Your mother was a stubborn one too."

"Before I forget, there's something Trevor said to me today—"

"Trevor Kilgore?" Nadine's voice turned razor sharp. "Where did you see him?"

"He and Barbara showed up at the reading of the will this morning, hoping that I wouldn't."

"How vile. That man is nothing but a money-grabbing idiot. What my sister sees in him, I'll never understand."

"He told me if it weren't for him, I'd be dead, and furthermore, that I 'owe' him. Do you have any idea why he'd say something like that to me?"

Nadine scoffed. "Pay no attention to that man. I'm sure it's just another one of his ploys to guilt a member of the family into giving him money. That is the one thing he excels at."

"I understand Victoria gave him a lot of money over the years. That's why there's very little cash left in the estate."

"It's tragic." Nadine leaned forward in her chair. "Please, dear, consider my offer. Do yourself a favor and return to Scotland without delay, before you find yourself drawn into the madness of this family. If you stay, I fear you'll soon wish you hadn't."

— 14 —

Coleen and Deborah returned soon after Nadine left. Before Coleen could assault Shannon with questions she wasn't ready to answer, she grabbed the keys to the truck and headed for the garage.

"I'm going to the inn to check us out. Do you want to come?" Shannon called out to Coleen.

"Yes." Confused, Coleen hurried to catch up to her. "I take it you don't want to talk about your lunch with Nadine?"

Shannon shook her head and Coleen dropped the subject.

They drove to town in silence to check out of the Apple Grove Inn. Betty was sorry to see them leave, but she told Shannon she looked forward to seeing her at the next meeting of the Purls.

Shannon unpacked her suitcase in her grandmother's room as soon as they returned to the mansion. She hung all of her outfits in the closet and stowed everything else in the dresser drawers. The last item she pulled from her suitcase was her husband's unfinished scarf, complete with knitting needles. She'd packed it as an afterthought. But now she was glad she'd brought the scarf along. It comforted her to have a reminder of John—of his strength and calm resolve—near her after the emotional turmoil of the day.

Shannon sighed. *My mother was crazy. And her mother locked her away. How could Dad allow that to happen?*

While the water filled the white clawfoot tub, Shannon turned her attention to the three apothecary jars on the counter. Desperate for something to calm her nerves, she filled a scoop with bath salts and smelled them. Tiny flecks of juniper and dried mint imparted a marvelous scent. She emptied the scoop into the bubbling water. Then she added a scoop of red rose petals into a small linen bag she found nearby and dropped it in the water as well.

She placed a hand towel and her grandmother's letter on the stand next to the tub. Then she slipped off her robe and sank into the bath to soak. The hot water released the fragrance in the rose petals and it soon filled the room. After soaking for a good while, Shannon felt as limp as a dishrag, her body finally relaxed.

"It's now or never," she muttered. She dried her fingers on the towel and reached for the envelope. After all she'd learned about her grandmother from Nadine, her enthusiasm about reading the letter had diminished significantly.

Handwritten with a beautiful flourish on fine linen, the first page of the letter contained only one paragraph, centered halfway down the page.

My Dearest Shannon:

Before you read any further, please be aware this letter is for your eyes only. It's paramount to your safety and the safety of your children that you do not share the information contained in this letter with anyone else.

She shuffled the pages, her curiosity growing.

I hope this day finds you well. If you're reading this, that means I have already departed from this world to my heavenly reward.

Though I only had the privilege of knowing you as a baby, my heart was always with you. I have followed your life with much joy, and am proud of you and what you have accomplished. I know the estate and the craft store will be in good hands.

As far as my attorney is concerned, those properties, plus a modest monetary stipend, are all I have left to will to you. It is my sincere hope you will be able to retain these and prosper. But I have made another provision for you and your children as well, a provision unknown to any other person.

In order to set aside an investment on your behalf with the last of my money, I made a private trip to New York when I first learned of my illness. On that trip, I purchased a necklace of rare pink diamonds in a titanium setting. As I write this letter, the appraised value of the piece is over $350,000.

No one else knows of the existence of the necklace. It's hidden on the grounds of the estate. The key to locating it is through the gift you should have received, or will soon receive. It is a posthumous gift from me to you, entrusted to my dear friends, Betty, Joyce, Kate, and Melanie.

I love you, my dearest Shannon. Please tell Alec and Lara I love them too.

Remember, no one else knows about this hidden treasure. If you tell anyone, be certain they are worthy of your trust. It would be to your advantage to destroy this letter, lest it fall into the wrong hands.

Blessings to you, my darling granddaughter.

Forever yours,

Victoria Paisley

The letter drifted down to the tile floor as Shannon's hands covered her face. The tears she'd held back for days now began to flow in a torrent. Emotions warred within her—sadness and anger, but more than anything, confusion. Her grandmother's letter made no mention of her mother or what she'd done to her. Why wouldn't she admit what she'd done? Was that why she bought the diamonds—to ease her guilty conscience?

No necklace could possibly atone for keeping a child separated from her mother. Though her father had done his level best to make her feel loved and secure, Shannon had gone through life feeling a deep sense of rejection. The loss of her mother hit her harder than anyone could have imagined. Through the years, she'd learned to hide her feelings. She kept her emotions in check, only to pour them out later through creative pursuits, an outlet she found soothing and purposeful.

She read and reread the letter again. Regardless of the reason for its purchase, she needed the money the necklace would bring in order to stay afloat while she got settled and turned the business around.

Shannon touched the locket around her neck, thinking of her mother. *At least now I finally know the truth.*

She dragged herself from the tub and curled up into a ball on the bed, ready for the day to end. But sleep eluded her. Something nagged at the back of her mind.

She couldn't shake the feeling that there was still more to the story.

* * *

"If I have to say something nice about this pile of scrap metal, it is roomy. I'll give it that much." Coleen settled into the front seat of the truck next to Shannon.

"You see? It's growing on you already. How was your morning on the town?" Shannon steered the truck away from the store.

"My morning was lovely. I sampled cakes and pastries at the Pink Sprinkles bakery. I visited with Kate at her dog grooming shop. Then I helped Melanie arrange flowers. After that, I visited with Betty at the inn. You really have a wonderful collection of new friends here. I approve of them wholeheartedly."

"Do you? So you think I should replace you, then?" Shannon teased.

"*Pish-posh*, you know full well it would take more than four of them to replace one of me."

Shannon laughed.

"How was your morning at the shop?" Coleen asked.

Shannon shook her head. "I'm afraid the store needs some of that TLC Michael mentioned."

"It did seem a bit neglected."

"That sums it up in a nutshell. The stockrooms are dirty and disorganized. My office is a mess. The interior of the shop is shabby. The walls need a coat of fresh paint. Upstairs, the loft area is filthy. The artists don't clean up after themselves, which surprises me, because some of them retail their work in their areas."

Coleen stared ahead at the road. "And what about the manager? She seemed a bit rough to me."

"She is. I've yet to get a complete list of all the supplies sold since Victoria's death. I requested it days ago. I suspect she was working with Barbara to sell off inventory and split the money. I'd like to let her go, but I'm not sure I can manage without her yet."

"Your new friends had a few things to say about how she's handled the store since Victoria fell ill."

"Oh?"

"Let's just say they weren't positive. I'd like to shower and change my clothes. Do you think Deborah will have lunch cooked for us?"

"I hope so."

Coleen nudged her side. "Isn't it splendid to have someone to care for you? I can't imagine anything nicer."

"I know I've said it before, but I'm still getting used to the idea. It's strange. One day I was struggling just to pay my bills. The next, I'd inherited a mansion and a business."

Shannon turned the truck onto the long drive leading to the mansion.

"The mansion's not that far from the store, is it?" Coleen looked back as if to gauge the miles. "Less than ten minutes. Of course, it takes another ten minutes just to navigate your driveway."

"Very funny."

Coleen studied her profile. "You need to laugh more. Processing all this news about your family and the burdens of the business is taking a toll on you."

Shannon tightened her grip on the wheel. She still hadn't told Coleen the latest news about her mom's mental illness and the hidden necklace. She preferred to let it sink in privately first.

"What do you suggest I do?" she asked her friend.

Coleen drummed her fingers on the dashboard. "Tomorrow, I think we should do something fun. Why don't I call Michael? I heard him mention something about hiking trails in the area. He'll know where we should go. Why, I'll bet if I asked him, he'd even take us hiking. What do you think?"

"No!" Shannon blurted. "I mean, don't bother him. I'm sure the last thing he'd be interested in doing is showing tourists how to hike along a coastline."

"I'd really like to go to the beach while we're here," Coleen pressed. "I did come halfway across the globe for you."

Shannon concentrated on the road, trying to ignore her friend's expectant stare. "Oh, very well. Call him. But you must promise me one thing."

"What?"

"No matchmaking funny business. I've told you how I feel about a relationship right now."

"For goodness, sake!" Coleen threw her hands up in a dramatic fashion in an attempt to hide her true intentions, an act Shannon saw right through. "It's just a hike."

Shannon pulled to a stop in front of the house and looked at her friend. "Uh-huh."

Half an hour later, Shannon wandered down to the pier on the lake and stopped at the edge, mentally forming a game plan to find the necklace. Coleen trailed behind, holding a glass of water filled with sliced strawberries. True to her word, the first thing Coleen had done upon their arrival was hop in the shower. Shannon, however, did not. She'd taken the opportunity to study the needlepoint gift from her grandmother, searching for any clue as to the location of the hidden necklace. So far, she'd drawn a blank.

Deborah had left out a pitcher filled with ice and strawberries, picked and sliced early that morning from the garden. Next to the pitcher, on a wooden tray, were an assortment of cheeses, crackers, and grapes. The snack helped stave off their appetites until lunch was ready.

The lake, calm and peaceful in the afternoon light, mirrored the blue of the sky and the puffy white clouds above. Insects pinged to and fro, skimming the surface of the water. Water lilies floated serenely, their white blooms contrasting with the green of the pads. A gentle breeze swayed the tall grasses and reeds along the banks.

Her eyes closed, Shannon took a deep breath. *I like it here.*

She tried to imagine the verdant fields of green grass back home, the misty moors, and the meadows dotted with wildflowers. She thought of the monoliths of stone she'd visited with John, the castles, towns, and villages like her own. The history that echoed through her soul.

But she no longer felt any kinship to the place. Her heart had undergone some sort of shift, the coastal town in one country replaced by a coastal town in another.

This is where I'm meant to be.

She opened her eyes and gazed out at the reflection of the clouds on the lake water. A metallic object in the midst of the reeds and grasses on the opposite bank caught her eye.

"Be right back," she told Coleen. Then she walked around the lake to the other side.

The object turned out to be a sign stuck to a skinny

wooden post. It rose from the water to the height of the vegetation surrounding the lake. White with black letters, it read, "Tall Grass."

Why on earth would Victoria bother to label the tall grass as such? Shannon looked around, but she didn't see any other plants or vegetation labeled.

Chalking it up to her grandmother's eccentricity she returned to the pier.

"What's over there?" Coleen asked.

"From what I can tell, a completely useless sign." Shannon lowered herself to a sitting position. She pulled the edge of her skirt upward, slid off her shoes, and dangled her legs in the cool water. "Ahh."

Coleen joined her. Rolling up her pants legs, she slipped her shoes off and tried the water with one toe. She promptly jerked it back out. "That's cold!"

Eyelids half-closed, Shannon breathed in and out, slow and calm. "It's wonderful. I can't remember when I've felt so relaxed."

Coleen gathered her resolve and plunked both legs in the water at once. "Very c-c-cold."

"You'll get used to it after a minute."

"I'm sure I will, after my feet go numb. By the way, I spoke to Michael."

Shannon's eyes snapped open. "Already?"

"Yep. Deborah gave me his number. We're on for a hike tomorrow morning."

Shannon struggled to sit up, her relaxed mood slipping away. "I'm surprised he could find the time during the work week on such short notice."

Coleen shrugged. "He's the one who suggested we go tomorrow. It sounded to me like he's genuinely looking forward to it."

"Hmm." Shannon closed her eyes again, closing the topic. Her mind returned to the necklace once more.

They soaked up the sun for a good twenty minutes before a loud bell clanged.

"Who's ringing a bell?" Coleen looked around.

"*Why* is someone ringing a bell?"

The bell continued to ring.

"I hope it means lunch is ready." Coleen clambered to her feet. "I'm starving."

Shannon shook her head. "When *aren't* you starving? I don't know how you stay so slim." She followed her eager friend back to the house.

Deborah waited for them outside the kitchen door, a teacher's hand bell in one hand. As they approached, she smiled. "Never fails."

"Am I to assume that's the dinner bell?" Coleen asked, her voice filled with hope.

"Sure is. Lunch bell, in this case."

"Why do you ring it?"

"Because it works." She winked and motioned for them to follow her to the breakfast room, where the table was set for three.

Shannon and Coleen sat down. Deborah stood by, watching.

"Shannon, I should have mentioned this to you before, but your grandmother and I were in the habit of taking our meals together. We ate our meals in separate rooms years ago, but we decided to dispense with that practice since it was only the two of us in this big house. I hope you don't mind, but I continued with the tradition."

Shannon motioned for Deborah to sit. "It's a sensible solution. I see no reason to change things."

Deborah smiled. "Thank you."

She sat down and asked them to pass their bowls her way. She lifted the cover from a white tureen and ladled homemade tomato soup into each bowl, sprinkling croutons on top before passing them back.

Then she passed around a small tray of grilled cheese sandwiches on slices of homemade bread dotted with freshly chopped rosemary. A spring salad rounded out the meal.

"So, Shannon, I haven't had the chance to ask you, how did your meeting with Nadine go yesterday?" Deborah asked.

"Fine." Shannon kept her eyes on her food.

"I'll bet it was interesting to talk to her and learn more about your family."

"Yes."

Coleen harrumphed. "I know you're hiding something, Shannon." She turned to Deborah. "I've gotten nothing but one-syllable answers out of her about it since last night."

Deborah frowned. "Did Nadine say something to upset you?"

Shannon looked up and saw the concern on their faces. "Actually, yes."

"What did she say?"

"She told me ..." Shannon paused, struggling to get the words out. "My mother had a multiple personality disorder and that's why she left us."

"What?" Coleen exclaimed.

"She said Victoria hid Beth away in a mental institution so she wouldn't bring shame upon the family. She died there, soon after."

For a few moments no one spoke.

"To be honest," Shannon continued. "I'm still in shock from the news. Of all the scenarios I'd created in my mind over the years as to why I had no mother, this wasn't one of them."

"Oh, Shannon, I'm so sorry. I don't know what to say." Coleen stood and gave her friend a hug. She turned to Deborah. "Can this be true?"

"I really can't say." Deborah got up and walked to the refrigerator. She pulled out a bottle of homemade salad dressing.

"I don't want to think about this right now." Shannon took a deep breath. "Let's move on to a more pleasant topic, shall we?"

Deborah returned to the table and sat down. An awkward silence followed.

Shannon tasted her soup. "Deborah, this is delicious, the best I've ever had. How did someone as talented as you come to work here?"

Clearly pleased by the compliment, Deborah's dour demeanor changed. She put down her spoon and looked at the two of them. "My sister, Gertrude, and I trained as chefs, but back when we were young, those jobs were hard to come by for women. Restaurants weren't interested in hiring female chefs. The only jobs we could get at the time were as cooks, working for individual households. I worked in five or six homes before settling here."

"So your sister worked in homes as well?" Shannon asked.

"At first, but she was more persistent than I was. Eventually she found a mom-and-pop restaurant in Cincinnati willing to take her on. The restaurant was a huge success. She worked there for many years."

"And now she's here, working at the inn?"

"Yes. When she decided to retire, Gertrude moved near me so we could spend more time together. I know it must seem odd, but neither of us ever married. Not that we didn't come close, mind you. But now all we have is each other."

"How did you come to work for my grandmother?" Shannon asked.

Deborah dabbed the corners of her mouth with a napkin. "She sampled my food at someone else's house and decided she wanted me to come and work for her."

"Because you were the best."

A flush bloomed across Deborah's face. "I wouldn't go that far."

"Well, *I* would." Coleen handed her bowl to the woman for seconds.

As she ladled soup into the bowl, Deborah glanced at Shannon. "There's something I want to ask you."

"What is it?" Shannon asked.

"I'm accustomed to speaking my mind, so forgive me for my directness, but I'd like to know if I can count on having a job or not. Are you planning to stay here in Apple Grove? And if so, are you going to keep me on?" She handed Coleen her bowl, careful not to spill any of the hot liquid. "Many years ago, your grandmother hired me as a cook. But over the course of time, I also began to manage the household and make sure things were kept tidy. We call in maids once a month for the deep cleaning. I'm getting too old to do that kind of work in a place this big. Of course, with an estate this large, we also have a part-time gardener who oversees the care of the grounds. I'm responsible for coordinating his schedule." She stopped to catch her breath. "I'm rambling."

Shannon clasped her cup with both hands. "I wish I had a straight answer for you, but I honestly don't know if I can afford to keep you on yet. I've only recently made up my mind to stay, and I haven't had time to dig into the finances."

"You've decided to stay?" Coleen dropped her spoon, splattering tomato soup onto the tablecloth.

"Yes. And I owe you an apology for not telling you sooner. I think I've managed to blurt it out to half the town. But I knew telling my dearest friend would be the hardest." She sighed. "I know this place has secrets and a past I may not like, but despite all that, I find there's something endearing about Apple Grove. I feel as if I've come home. And the best part is the twins plan to join me once this semester is over. They're going to attend Portland University next year."

Deborah clasped her hands. "I'm so glad. Victoria would be very happy to hear you say that."

"I'm happy for you too. I've told you all along you should, should ..." Coleen picked up her napkin and dabbed at her eyes. "Stay here."

"Please don't cry." Shannon felt a lump form in her throat. "I can't bear it. I know my life is changing, and things won't ever be the same, but—"

"No, your life will be better. *Much* better," Coleen choked out between tears. "I'm being selfish. Missing you already. That part won't be easy." She reached across the table to grasp Shannon's hand. "But you'll be happy here. I know you will."

"I'm so glad I have your support in this. I couldn't do it without you," Shannon said. "I plan to change my return flight home. I'll fly back at the semester's end. That way, the kids and I can go through the house together, pack things up, and put it on the market."

"I'll keep an eye on it for you until then."

"Thank you." Shannon turned to Deborah. "I hope I'll be able to afford to keep you on. My grandmother left me a modest amount of money. My first order of business is to get the craft store back on track and operating at a profit."

"I understand," Deborah said.

Shannon looked around. "But I don't know what I'd do without you, or the gardener. There is no possible way I could keep up a home of this size by myself while running the store."

Deborah smiled, the creases beside her mouth forming small accordions. "You'll find a way. I sense you have the same drive for success Victoria had. There wasn't anything she couldn't do once she set her mind to it. I won't pack my bags just yet."

"Where would you go if you left?" Coleen asked.

Deborah shrugged. "I don't know. I haven't thought about that for decades. Truth is, there's nowhere else I'd *want* to go." She looked around. "I consider this place my home."

Shannon was hit by the magnitude of the woman's simple statement. Deborah really didn't have anyplace else to go. She had no husband or children. She'd lived full time at the estate for more than thirty years.

Shannon cleared her throat. "I've made up my mind, Deborah. Don't even *think* about packing your bags. You're staying. We'll find a way to make it work."

— 15 —

Harold Giddings could only be described as an unusual character. When Morgan showed him to the stockroom, Shannon had to do a double take to believe her own eyes. He appeared to be in his late sixties. And, truth be told, he appeared to be a child of the *late sixties*. An untrimmed beard sprouted from his chin, and a long braid of gray hair entwined with feathers hung down the back of his neck. Dressed in faded jeans, a plaid shirt with the sleeves cut off, and worn sandals, his appearance epitomized the era.

He held out his hand. "Shannon? I hope you don't mind, but I like to call folks by their first names."

"Not at all. It's nice to meet you, Harold." She motioned toward her friend. "This is Coleen. She's my best friend. I'm going to have her sit in on today's lesson."

He tipped his head toward Coleen. "Call me Harry, please. That's what my friends call me."

He set down a large black case that resembled a doctor's bag and surveyed the room. "Is this the place you want to use as a workroom?"

"That was my plan."

He stroked his scraggly beard. "I hope you've got a Plan B, because this room has no ventilation. It won't work."

"We need ventilation?"

"For the gases."

"Gases?" Coleen edged away from the black case.

He nodded. "To melt the silver solder. Can't do silversmithing without soldering."

Shannon drew her hands together. "Let's take a tour. Maybe we can spot the perfect place for a workshop together."

Harry smiled. "Let's go."

The three of them walked from one stockroom to the next, then to her office, and finally, upstairs to the loft areas. As they passed Morgan in the hall, Shannon felt her blood pressure rise. The woman had yet to produce the complete list of sold items Shannon had requested days before. All she'd come up with so far was a piece of paper with three items on it, stating it was a "partial" list. Her defiance was unfathomable. Shannon knew she needed to find someone to replace her, and fast.

"None of these places will work," Harry said. "What about out back?"

They moved to the small patio outside the back door. In the middle of it, a bright green picnic table marked the designated area for employee breaks.

Harry sat down at the table, a pleased look on his face. "This is perfect."

"But it's outside," Shannon argued.

"Well ventilated though." Coleen winked.

Harry nodded. "My thoughts exactly."

"Are you sure this is the best location?" Shannon looked around. "People passing by might see us."

Harry lifted his palms to the sky. "They might see artisans at work. Is that such a bad thing?"

Finger to her lips, Shannon thought a moment. "No, I suppose not."

"Besides," he added, "I'll be teaching you in the mornings before you open. There won't be too many people around."

"Good point," Shannon said. "What do we do first?"

Harry let the bag drop to the table and grinned broadly, revealing a large gap between his front teeth. "An eager student—I like that. Let's get down to business and see if you're cut out to be a silversmith. Remember our bargain?"

"I do." Shannon nodded. "Let's get started."

* * *

"No matter what you do, you gotta have flux on it." Harry pointed to the container.

Flux, a white acid paste, was to be painted on the metal first. According to her new teacher, the solder would not work without it.

For the past hour, Harry had been instructing Shannon and Coleen on the basics of silversmithing. Although she noticed Coleen yawning at times, Shannon was eager to learn, and she interrupted his instruction with dozens of questions. Harry didn't seem to mind, however. He answered each question patiently and in detail.

Shannon learned that she must use silver solder to attach designs to metal. The solder melted at a lower temperature than the metal. And she would have to purchase sheets of silver, copper, and brass in different thicknesses from which to cut her designs.

Then, there was the matter of which gas to use. Harry explained that butane was commonly used for thinner metals. But some people used a combination of acetylene and butane because it heated faster. That combination, however, was unstable and downright dangerous, according to Harry. He told them he favored a mixture of oxygen and propane for soldering. Though it took longer to come up to the desired heat, the combination was cleaner and safer than the other forms.

Before they began the hands-on lesson, he handed both women goggles, sharing horror stories about people who'd been disfigured because they didn't take appropriate safety precautions.

"I once knew a fella who lost an eye doing this stuff. Thought he was too manly to wear goggles. Told me goggles were for wimps. He changed his tune after the accident. A piece of metal flew up from the polishing cylinder and took his right eye."

"That's horrible," Shannon said. "What about the gas? How worried do I need to be about the possibility of an explosion?"

"You need to make sure you're using the correct gas for the job. I knew a gal who was always looking for shortcuts. She started experimenting with unstable gas mixtures. Unstable mixtures heat up fast, and you *can* get the job done in half the time. But you also run a huge risk of explosion. It could kill you or mess you up pretty bad."

"What happened to your friend?"

He ran his hands over the top of his head and exhaled. "Let's just say she won't be winning any beauty contests. But she is lucky to be alive."

Shannon heard Coleen gulp.

"I, um, don't think I want to make anything," Coleen said. "Would you mind if I do a little shopping and socializing instead?"

Shannon smiled at her friend. "Go right ahead. We'll meet up for lunch. How about that seafood place down the street?"

"Perfect. That's exactly what I was thinking. See you later." Coleen patted Harry on the back. "You're a nice man. Thank you for taking Shannon under your wing. Sorry I'm a disappointment as a student."

"That's OK." He smiled. "You're one cool lady, just not cut out to be a silver artisan. But I think we've answered the question as to whether or not Shannon's cut out for it."

"We have?" Shannon asked, hopeful.

"I can tell you're pretty excited about all this."

Shannon put down the pen and paper she was using to take notes. "Is it that obvious?" She bit her lip. "I have to confess, I've never been more excited. This is the most exhilarating work I've ever undertaken."

"You have a passion for it." He pointed at her with the flux brush. "I can see it in your eyes. Good. That's what I look for in a student."

"I'm assuming you won't be asking to buy back the equipment any time soon?" Shannon asked.

"The equipment is yours. I have no interest in buying it back."

Coleen went on her way to explore the town and visit their new friends. Harry went out to his truck. When he returned, he was carrying three sheets of metal, one of

40-grade silver, one of brass, and the other, copper. Using special scissors, Shannon would cut her designs from the silver and either brass or copper, and then solder the pieces together. She already had a design in mind: a silver cross with a heart of shiny brass in the center. She cut the pieces from the metal sheets.

Next, she painted the cross and heart with flux and positioned the heart in the center of the cross. Harry ignited the torch. Adrenaline pumping, Shannon made sure she was wearing her goggles correctly. Then, holding the cross in a pair of pliers, she applied the torch to the metal and soldered the heart in place.

"Now drop it in the pickling pot," Harry instructed.

The "pickling pot" was a simple slow cooker filled with a mixture of water and boric acid. When they had set it up before she started cutting out the metal designs, he'd explained that each piece would have to rest in the pickling pot for thirty minutes or longer to clean off the oxides.

"Now we wait," he said.

"Good. This will give me a chance to ask you a question I've wondered about all morning."

"Oh?"

"How did you get started as a silversmith?"

Harry's eyes took on a faraway look. "It was back in the sixties ..."

— 16 —

Later that evening, Shannon waited what seemed like forever until everyone retired to their own bedrooms. Once the house was finally quiet, she set about trying to figure out the location of the hidden necklace. She'd need the framed needlepoint if she hoped to make any headway, and Deborah had already hung it in the study.

She slipped Victoria's letter into her robe pocket and dug a tiny reading penlight out of her purse. She didn't want to flip on any more lights than necessary as she made her way to the study.

Holding the light high in one hand, she opened the bedroom door swiftly to avoid creaking and closed it in the same manner.

A gasp escaped her lips as she turned the corner from the hallway to the open landing. Through a skylight, moonlight sparkled on a marble statue of a Roman woman. As she passed it, Shannon noted the hollows of the eyes, impassive yet realistic in the surreal light.

With the help of the moonlight, she descended the stairs in her bare feet, the cool marble sending a shiver through her. She drew her robe up near her neck and headed for the study.

She managed to click the pocket door shut with nary a sound. She switched on a lamp and spotted the needlepoint on the wall near the worktable.

Her mouth formed the words as she tried to decipher meanings and uncover any hidden entendres.

Blessing For A New Home
A blessing upon your new home,
A blessing upon your new hearth,
A blessing upon your new dwelling,
Upon your newly kindled fire,

She stopped at the fifth line. After going round and round in her mind, considering possible ideas, she decided she'd be more comfortable if she took the needlepoint to her bedroom to ponder.

As she lifted it from the wall, she heard a noise that sounded like glass splintering.

The hair rose on her arms. *The needlepoint will have to wait.*

She started to exit the room, but stopped abruptly. *What if I encounter a thief?* Looking behind her, she noticed a pair of long needle-nose pliers poking out of a beading basket, and grabbed them. Leaving the study door ajar, she slipped into the foyer, hugging the wall. In spite of the cold tiles, she was thankful to be in bare feet, as it aided in her attempt to be stealthy.

The pocket door to the drawing room was closed. She pressed one ear against it but heard nothing. She turned her attention to the dining room. That door was closed as well. She listened against it, and her pulse quickened when she heard a rustling sound coming from within.

She stood frozen in place for a moment, uncertain of what to do. Logically, she knew it could be Deborah or Coleen, but her instinct warned her it wasn't. No light showed beneath the door; someone was creeping about in the dark, and that didn't seem like something either woman would do. She remembered that there was another way into the dining room, through the butler's pantry via the kitchen. She started in that direction.

Clutching the pliers in her hand, she crept through the kitchen. Moonlight streamed in from the bank of windows, enabling her to find her way with relative ease to the butler's pantry. From there, the path was dark and windowless. She kept close to the cabinetry, feeling her way along the cold granite counter until she reached the door to the dining room. It stood slightly ajar, but her eyes could make out nothing in the darkened room.

She heard someone moving about in the room, bumping into things, rattling glass and dishes. With her hand on the light switch, she counted to three, then flipped on the light and shoved the door open.

A figure clad in dark pants and shirt with a black ski mask stood near the fireplace.

Shannon let loose a bloodcurdling scream.

Startled at first, the figure paused, then lunged at her. The intruder grabbed her left arm with a grip so strong, she knew instinctively it had to be a man.

She screamed again, fighting against his grip. Then she remembered the pliers in her hand, and she plunged them into his shoulder.

He howled in pain just as Deborah and Coleen threw open the pocket doors on the other side of the room.

Deborah held a pistol trained on the intruder. "I've already called the cops." Her voice was deadly calm.

At that, the intruder bolted from the dining room, leaving a trail of blood. He tried to open the front door, but it was locked, and in his frantic state, he couldn't get it open. Like a caged animal, he leaped first to the right and then to the left, trying to stay out of Deborah's line of fire. Then he darted back into the dining room and headed for the bay windows.

Shattered glass glittered on the floor near the bank of windows. With the aid of heavy boots, he kicked out what was left of the glass and lowered his body through the opening.

Coleen raced to Shannon's side. "Are you all right?"

"I-I think so." Shaking, Shannon lowered herself to the floor and placed her head between her knees.

Deborah hurried to open the front door and look out. The sound of a motor zooming down the long drive told them all that whoever had been snooping around the house had come via automobile.

Coleen stooped down to comfort Shannon.

"Is she OK?" Deborah asked, coming to her side.

"She's shaking. I think she might be going into shock." Coleen patted Shannon's shoulder and tried to soothe her. "Breathe."

"I'll be right back." Deborah disappeared through the butler's pantry and returned a minute later with a towel she'd soaked in warm water. "Here, put this on her forehead. It'll help."

With the warmth of the towel and the calm breathing, Shannon began to feel more like herself—and just in time, for at that moment, the sound of sirens tore through the night.

Two police cars screeched to a stop in the circular drive. Deborah went to meet them at the door. Shannon heard her explaining what had happened.

She zeroed in on the sound of police radios, tinny voices communicating back and forth, and the voices of two men. Coleen left her side to fetch her a glass of water.

Deborah returned and helped Shannon to a chair. "Here she is. Poor thing was overcome."

"I don't know why this affected me so much," Shannon said. "I guess it's a culmination of everything that's happened this week. It's all starting to get to me. There's no need to make a fuss, though. I'll be fine."

She saw the look of concern on the policeman's face as he approached.

"Ma'am, I'm Chief Jack Grayson of the Apple Grove Police Department, and this is Officer Steve Brownley. I believe we saw you ladies at the Apple Grove Inn the other night." His eyes were focused on her robe. "Are you hurt?"

"I don't think so." She caught sight of her reflection in a mirror. Her robe was splattered with blood. She gasped. "Oh, no, no, no!"

The sight of the blood triggered raw panic in her, a panic she couldn't seem to control. Her breathing came fast as her heart pounded against her rib cage.

"It's OK." Deborah held her head against her shoulder. "You're safe."

Shannon struggled to pull herself together. "I stabbed him."

The chief flipped out a notepad. "Where?"

"In the shoulder."

"Which shoulder?"

Shannon replayed the attack in her mind. "The left one."

He glanced around. "With what?"

"A pair of long needle-nose pliers I use for beading."

"Are they still in here somewhere?" Officer Brownley asked.

"Here." Chief Grayson put on a glove and reached down to pick up her green-handled pliers off the carpet.

Officer Brownley produced a plastic bag marked "Evidence," and the chief dropped the pliers into the bag.

Coleen appeared with the glass of water in hand. A horrified expression crossed her face as she noticed the amount of blood spattered across the front of Shannon's robe.

"Oh, my." She stumbled slightly.

Officer Brownley pulled out a chair and helped her into it. Instead of handing the water to Shannon, she took a long sip herself.

The chief put his hand on Shannon's shoulder. "Mrs. McClain," he said softly. "I have a few more questions to ask if you're up to it."

The shock was wearing off. Shannon felt more like herself again. "Of course."

The chief got busy asking questions while Brownley gathered evidence near the broken window and around the room.

"You say you were in the study and you heard a strange sound. So you decided to investigate?"

"That's correct."

"Why didn't you call the police?"

She pointed upward. "My cellphone was upstairs, and I don't know where the phones are in this house yet. I decided to have a look for myself. I kept thinking about the car, the note ..."

Grayson held up a hand. "Wait a minute. What's this about a car?"

"I suspect the brake failure in my rental car earlier this week was no accident."

The chief scribbled on his notepad. "And what about a note?"

"Two notes, actually. Back home, right after I received the attorney's letter telling me I was heir to Victoria's home and business, a threatening note was left on my door."

"What did it say?"

Coleen answered. "It said, 'Stay away from Apple Grove, or else.'"

He turned from Coleen back to Shannon. "Is that correct?"

"Yes."

"And what did the other note say?"

"'Leave.'"

The chief looked up from his notepad. "You mean the note left on the mirror at the Apple Grove Inn?"

"Yes. I believe it was meant for me. Someone was trying to intimidate me so I'd leave town. I thought once Victoria's will was read, all the harassment would end."

"OK, back to the present. After you discovered the intruder this evening, what happened?"

"He lunged at me and grabbed my arm."

"How do you know the intruder was a male?" Grayson asked.

"He—the intruder—was very strong. I felt his grip."

The chief examined her arm. Shannon was surprised to see a red welt starting to form, one that would likely turn into a nasty bruise.

"And that's when you stabbed him, the intruder?"

"Yes, in the shoulder."

"You're either a very brave or a very foolish woman, Mrs. McClain." Grayson pointed at her with his pencil. "Next time, do yourself a favor, and call us instead."

She nodded.

"I have no idea what to make of the note you received back home or how it might relate to tonight's attempted burglary," the chief said.

"I'll bet I know the connection," Deborah interrupted. "It's the Kilgore family. They've been trying to get their hands on Victoria's things since the day she died. That's why I keep the doors locked day and night. I don't trust them."

Chief Grayson took off his hat and rubbed his head.

"Do you know them?" Shannon asked him.

"I do," he said.

She searched his face. "Are they as awful as everyone says?"

He sighed and put his hat back on. Instead of answering Shannon, he addressed Deborah. "Have they asked you for specific items?"

"They want everything, including the house. It's no secret. For the two years Victoria was sick, they came by every week, asking her—*begging* her—for something."

"And what did she give them?"

"Money." Deborah frowned. "She'd give them money.

Victoria was determined to leave everything else to Shannon."

The chief signaled Brownley with a sideways glance. "Let's pay the Kilgores a visit."

He turned to Shannon. "Mrs. McClain, I suggest you try to get some sleep. We'll keep an eye on the area tonight and stop by again tomorrow."

Deborah walked them to the door and locked it behind them. Then, she returned to the dining room. "I'll have the window fixed tomorrow. In the meantime, I think I have a large piece of cardboard in the attic we can use to cover it."

"I'll help you find it." Coleen gave Shannon a worried glance and followed Deborah from the room.

As soon as they were gone, Shannon pounded her fists on the table, angry she'd let a criminal get under her skin.

She glanced around the room, surveying the damage. The lids to three of the tureens were off, several drawers on the buffet hung open, and two vases were overturned. But nothing appeared to be missing.

It was as if the intruder was looking for something specific.

A chill rippled through her.

Someone else knows about the necklace.

* * *

The next day, Shannon shuffled into the breakfast room, still in her white silk gown and robe, only to find Deborah and Coleen already seated at the table, coffee cups in hand. Both women had dark circles under their eyes from lack of sleep.

Deborah's hair was up in rollers, and Coleen's hadn't even been combed. Shannon had already seen what she looked like in the bathroom mirror, she knew it wasn't pretty.

The peaceful feeling of the house had been replaced by a breathless fear, a pump of adrenaline sparked by the intrusion.

"Good morning." Deborah got up and wrapped her arms around Shannon. "You OK? I made some scrambled eggs."

Shannon shook her head. "I'm not hungry, but thank you."

"You need to eat," Coleen fussed. "Now sit yourself down. Deborah brewed some coffee, but if you prefer tea ..."

"Coffee will be fine."

"I'll get you a cup."

"And I'll get you some breakfast." Deborah scuttled away in her slippers. "No arguments. You have to eat."

Shannon smiled. The two were clucking over her as if she were a child.

"Here you go." Coleen set a cup of coffee in front of her just as Deborah returned with her food.

The doorbell rang. They all looked up.

"Maybe that's Chief Grayson." Shannon started to get up, but Deborah waved her away.

"Sit. Eat. I'll get it."

As she walked away, Coleen brought her hands to her temples. "Oh no."

Her fork poised in midair, Shannon stared at her friend. "Why don't I like the sound of that?"

Coleen grimaced in an apologetic pose. "In all the excitement, I ..."

A man's voice echoed through the house.

"... I forgot to call Michael and cancel."

Deborah's approaching footsteps echoed in the hall, followed by the heavier footsteps of a man. Shannon gulped down her forkful of eggs, ran a hand through her hair, and drew her robe tight around her. Coleen did likewise.

Michael appeared in the doorway. He wore a long-sleeved blue cotton shirt, hiking shorts, socks, and rugged boots. His hair looked a bit disheveled, giving him a boyish air.

In as pleasant a voice as Shannon could muster, she greeted him. "Good morning."

He arched a brow. "Am I early?"

"No, we're late," Coleen said. "We had a bit of drama here last light."

"What sort of drama?"

"Someone broke into the house," Deborah answered. "Shannon discovered the intruder and stabbed him in the shoulder with a pair of pliers."

Michael's expression turned dark. "Did you get a good look at him?"

"No," Shannon replied. "He wore a ski mask."

"But you're certain it was a man?"

"Yes." She lifted her sleeve to show him her bruised arm. "The grip felt like a man's grip, strong."

He turned to Deborah. "Did Grayson come?"

She nodded. "And Brownley."

"Did they keep the house under surveillance last night?"

"Yes. They left early this morning."

Michael raked a hand through his hair, clearly distraught. "Shannon, you need to have the locks changed and a security system installed."

She blinked, taken aback by his harsh tone.

"I agree," she said. "I planned to talk to Deborah about it this morning."

"No, it won't get done fast enough that way. I can have it done today, and at a low cost, by people I know to be trustworthy. It's important that you do this immediately."

Shannon furrowed her brows. *Why is he barking orders at me?*

"You'd be wise to take that deal," Deborah said. "Michael's firm is known far and wide for their security work. Your grandmother trusted him."

Shannon met his gaze, recalling what Deborah had told her about his wife's death. His grandmother *did* hire him to keep her safe. The least she could do was let him try. "All right then. I'll take you up on your offer."

"Good." He studied her face, his expression and demeanor softening. "Are you OK?"

"I'm a little tired, that's all."

"But not too tired for a hike, right?" Coleen interrupted. "I could use a walk after all the stress of last night."

Deborah tapped Michael on the arm. "Call your people and have them come over. I'll be here to let them in. You take the girls on the hike and have a good time."

"I shouldn't leave—"

"No arguments, Michael. You can monitor the progress by phone. I packed the lunches last night before I went to bed. Nothing too fancy, mind you. But everything's ready to go."

Coleen stood up. "I can be ready in ten minutes."

Shannon tipped back the rest of her coffee. "Give me fifteen."

Deborah ushered Michael to a chair. "While you're waiting, you can eat. I'll fix you a plate."

Michael didn't bother to argue.

Coleen and Shannon excused themselves and hurried upstairs. As Shannon exchanged her nightclothes for shorts and a T-shirt, she looked around in vain for her tennis shoes. She finally located them in a special compartment of her suitcase.

She was about to leave the room when she remembered Victoria's letter, still in her robe pocket.

"Yoo-hoo. Are you ready yet?" Coleen called through the door.

"Just a minute." She pulled the letter from her robe, folded it in half and shoved it far under her mattress. Then she opened her bedroom door. "Let's go."

— 17 —

Shannon and Coleen stood with Michael in the parking lot at the entrance to the trail that would lead them to the beach.

"I chose Silver Sands because it's a good beginner trail," Michael explained.

Shannon read the trail sign and laughed. "I'll say it's a beginner trail. It's only two miles."

He leaned on the trail marker, an amused look on his face. "Don't forget, we'll be walking a good distance once we reach the beach."

Coleen smiled and hoisted her backpack. "Let's go."

After less than a minute of walking, the scenery changed so much that Shannon felt like they'd entered a different world. In the deep shade of tree cover, fern fronds the height of her waist curled along the edge of the trail. Ancient trees, thick and gnarled with branches, lined the way, blanketing the path in shade. The trail sloped steadily downward, coiling to the left, then to the right.

A massive trunk with a hollow big enough to hold two people caught Shannon's attention.

"Wait," she called to the others. "Could we get a picture, please?"

Michael volunteered to take the picture, so Shannon handed him her camera. Coleen joined her in the tree hollow, though Shannon could tell she was a bit nervous.

"What's wrong?"

"I dunno, I guess standing in a rotting tree trunk makes me feel a bit squeamish and creepy crawly." Coleen fluffed her hair and pinched her cheeks. "Can you hurry up and take the picture?"

"Will do." Michael snapped two photos and handed the camera back to Shannon.

"Aaah!" Coleen screamed.

"What is it?"

Coleen pointed at a giant yellow slug inching its way up the hollow of the tree near her head.

Michael laughed. "That's a banana slug."

Her friend doubled over to catch her breath. "It's horrid."

"It does resemble a banana," Shannon said. "Look—it even has some brown spots, like a ripe one."

But Coleen refused to look at the creature. Rolling her eyes, Shannon bent to pick up her gear.

"Not so fast." Coleen grabbed Michael's sleeve and guided him toward the hollow. She beckoned to Shannon, who responded with a stern look of warning. "I want to take a picture of you two in the tree. Hold steady."

Shannon glared at her friend. *I'm going to kill her.* But she played along with Coleen's not-so-subtle ploy and joined Michael in the tree.

Coleen motioned at them as she looked through the viewfinder. "Closer, closer. I can't fit you both in the picture unless you scooch in close together."

On second thought, I'm going to kill her... slowly.

Shannon knew full well what Coleen was doing. She

only hoped Michael didn't. He had an amused look on his face, so she decided to go along with her friend's request. They moved in close together, and she felt his arm move across her back. The light caress of his fingers on her shoulder made her breath catch.

"Got it." Coleen looked up from the lens. "Thank you both."

Shannon bolted from the tree to put some distance between them. Then she picked up her gear and resumed walking.

Half an hour later, they crossed a footbridge and suddenly found themselves bathed in bright sunshine. The surroundings had changed once again, and the trail had brought them into a completely different world. Tall grasses sprinkled with wildflowers lined the path. Shannon spotted a rabbit nibbling some tender shoots. She nudged Coleen just in time to see the rabbit hop off into the foliage. The trail flattened out and they stepped out to view a breathtaking vista.

They walked atop a cliff overlooking a long, wide beach, all the while captivated by the crash of the waves over the gray sand below. Gargantuan trees lined the edge of the cliff, their limbs twisted into impossible contortions by the wind.

The women followed Michael to the edge and looked down.

The cliff was perhaps twenty or thirty feet off the beach. A sloping path studded with large boulders and rocks was cut short by a pile of massive logs, which met the sandy path leading down to the beach.

Shannon shifted her gaze to the waves, feeling the wind lift her hair. How truly at home she felt. Wind, wave, and water were a lullaby to her spirit, especially after the events of the previous night.

Michael's cellphone rang. "Excuse me." He walked a few steps away to talk.

Shannon turned to Coleen and fixed her with a look.

Coleen opened her eyes wide, all innocence. "What?" she mouthed.

"I'm on to you," Shannon whispered.

"I have no idea what you're referring to." Coleen looked out at the water. "Isn't it lovely?"

Shannon saw Michael hang up, and she dropped the subject.

"That was Deborah," Michael said. "The security company is there. They've already started. She said Grayson stopped by too. He paid a visit to the Kilgores first thing this morning. Unfortunately, the visit proved to be a dead end. They've checked everyone in the family for a shoulder injury with the exception of your cousin Fritz, whom they claim is out of the country. None of them has a visible puncture wound."

Shannon nodded. "Was that all the chief had to say?"

"For now," Michael answered. "But don't despair. He's stubborn. He won't give up."

"Good. That's comforting to know."

"Do we have to walk across those logs?" Coleen interrupted, pointing down the trail.

Michael looked ahead. "We do."

Coleen groaned.

"I was under the impression this trail was too easy for you," he teased.

"I may have spoken too soon."

They continued on, stepping gingerly over boulders, balancing on long wooden logs, and then navigating large, bluish-gray stones. When they reached the sand, they headed to the middle of the beach and settled in near a massive log.

Michael took off his hiking boots and waded out into the ocean a short distance. Shannon and Coleen stayed at the water's edge, the waves washing over their feet and ankles, sometimes splashing up to their knees.

Shannon watched as the waves hit the beach and then pulled backward. The glossy wet sand reflected back at her like a mirror.

She turned to her friend. "The water is invigorating, isn't it?"

"I believe the word you're looking for is frigid."

"I think you've gone soft since your arrival into the States," Shannon joked. "Where's the hearty Scotswoman I once knew?"

"She's right here, thinking that she can't feel her feet anymore." Coleen glanced at Michael and lowered her voice. "You have to admit, the man looks good in the wilderness, all rugged and ... primitive."

"I admit nothing. And I refuse to get pulled into this conversation." But even as she uttered the words, Shannon realized with a start that she'd already made the same observations.

They walked back to the log, and Shannon unpacked

their picnic lunch from her backpack. Michael joined them a short while later, and they all dug into the excellent lunch Deborah had prepared for them.

When she finished her sandwich, Coleen jumped up. "I'm going for a walk," she announced. "You two keep eating. No need to rush on my account."

She took off down the beach before Shannon could respond.

Michael watched her walk away. "Your friend is charming. I'll bet you're really going to miss her when she leaves."

"I am. It's going to be so—wait a minute, how did you know I plan to stay in Apple Grove?"

"Deborah mentioned it." He smiled. "News travels fast in our little town."

"It certainly does. I guess it shouldn't surprise me. I come from a town about the same size as Apple Grove, and I've found my neighbors often know more about my business than I do." She took a sip from a can of green tea. "Anyway, to answer your question, yes, I'll miss her sorely."

He leaned back on his left elbow and winced.

"Are you hurt?"

"It's nothing. Strained muscle is all." He redistributed his weight onto his other arm. "So, since you're from Scotland, you might be able to answer something I've often wondered about."

Shannon feigned dismay. "Not another question about why Scotsmen wear 'skirts'?"

He paused. "No. But now that you mention it, it is a good question. What I'd like you to tell me is, what exactly is *haggis*?"

Shannon drew her knees together and rested her arms on top. "The best way to explain haggis is to have you try some. But since I don't have any to offer you, I suppose a description will have to suffice. Once you hear what it is, though, you'll probably never sample it."

"It's a risk I'm willing to take."

"Well, *haggis* is a traditional Scottish dish containing minced sheep's heart, liver, and lungs, onion, oatmeal, suet, spices, salt, and stock, all mixed together. Then it's simmered in the animal's stomach for three hours."

His face betrayed no reaction akin to the look of disgust she'd expected. "And you actually eat this dish?"

"I do."

"Do you like it?"

She reclined onto her side as well. "No one's ever asked me that. We just eat it."

He waited, his blue eyes twinkling.

"Oh, all right. No, I don't particularly like it."

He laughed. "Then why do you eat it?"

"Tradition, I suppose. It's a vital component of the Burns supper."

"What's that?"

"A supper of *haggis*, *neeps* and *tatties*. Then there's the reading of the poem, 'Address to a Haggis,' by Robert Burns, of course."

"Who's he? And what are *neeps,* and *tatties*?" He cringed. "I'm almost afraid to hear the answer."

"Don't tell me you haven't heard of Burns. He's *only* one of Scotland's most beloved poets."

"And the *neep* things, what are those?"

Annoyed, she blurted, "Mashed turnips."

"Sounds delicious. Whenever I get a craving for sheep's innards, I always make sure to have some mashed turnips on the side—and *tatties*, too, whatever those are."

"Mashed potatoes."

"Now *that's* a dish I'd enjoy."

She shook her head. "I still can't believe you've never heard of Burns."

He grinned. "Actually, I've heard of him. A long time ago, back in high school or college, I remember reading some of his poetry."

"Well then, perhaps there's hope for you yet." Shannon picked up a handful of sand and let it sift between her fingers.

"Listen, Shannon," Michael began. "I know you've had a difficult time this past week."

She smiled warily. "That's ... an understatement."

"You're probably wondering who you can really trust in this town."

Shannon remained silent.

"I hope you know you can trust me," he continued. "I'm always here if you need help, with anything."

"Thank you."

Shannon searched his face, gauging the sincerity of his words. Michael carried many secrets, of that she was certain. But he also had a genuine quality about him that put her at ease.

A strong gust of salty sea air whipped around them. It caught a lock of Shannon's hair and flipped it over her head. Before she could react Michael reached out and brushed it back from her face.

She sucked in her breath at the touch of his fingers. Without a word, he continued his light caress down to her jawbone, cupping her face in his hand.

Warning bells clanged in her mind. But she couldn't pull away. Something in his molten gaze rendered her immobile.

He leaned toward her and she closed her eyes, her heart slamming against her ribcage. He was murmuring something, and she tried to listen. *What is he saying?*

"Shannon," he said, "you have to tell me."

Her eyelids fluttered open. "Tell you ...?"

"You have to tell me where the necklace is."

Tell him *what*? Shannon wrenched herself away in horror and stared at the man she'd dared to trust. "I-I don't know what you're talking about."

"I think you do. You have to tell me where it is. If you don't, they could kill you."

Not Michael too! The disappointment and fear Shannon felt was almost palpable. *How could I be so foolish?*

She jumped up and staggered away. "We'll find our own ride home. Don't you ever come near me again, do you understand? Not ever! Or I *will* call the police."

* * *

The ride home was a silent one. Sensing the tension in the air, Deborah didn't ask why they'd needed her to come pick them up. Or what had become of Michael.

They arrived home at about one-thirty, and Shannon immediately retired to her room to take a quick shower and decompress in private. After drying her hair into curls, she donned a comfortable pair of black tights and a long, cream-colored shirt. As an afterthought, she added a leopard print scarf, tying it in a loose knot around her neck.

She checked her email. She discovered Morgan had finally forwarded the "complete" list of equipment sold since Victoria's passing, but she'd failed to include the selling price or the buyer's contact information. *She's playing games. I'm letting her go this week.* Pushing the problem out of her mind for the moment, Shannon pulled out the letter from under her mattress, tucked it into her pocket, and went to her friend's room.

She knocked on the door.

"Who is it?"

"A big, angry banana slug."

"That's not funny." The door swung open. Dressed in a pair of shorts and a white cotton blouse, Coleen looked relaxed and refreshed.

"I need to talk to you about something." Shannon breezed past her and settled into a wingback chair in front of the fireplace.

"Are you finally going to enlighten me on why we're no longer speaking to Michael?"

"You'll understand in a minute."

Coleen sank into the opposite chair. "You're scaring me a little. You look so serious."

Shannon handed her the letter. "Read it."

While Coleen read the letter, Shannon looked around the room, observing all of the special touches Victoria had employed. A pair of authentic Dutch boy shoes were displayed on the wall. A collection of blue willow plates in different sizes hung over the fireplace. A blue toile bedspread trimmed in white pompoms covered the bed. And the light blue and aqua polka dots on the white curtains filtered the sunlight, giving the room a unique glow.

Coleen looked up from the letter. "We have to find it."

Shannon smiled. "I hoped you'd say that. Contrary to my grandmother's wishes, I knew I had to tell you. You're my best friend. I know I can trust you."

"Of course you can, and of course I'll help you." Coleen tapped her chin with her finger. "Betty wasn't kidding when she said your grandma loved puzzles and riddles. This is a very cryptic way to lead you to your inheritance. And then there's Michael. I don't understand how he could possibly know about the necklace."

"I'm starting to think someone in the attorney's office is a snitch."

Coleen sighed. "It's hard for me to believe Michael is a bad guy. What if he really is trying to help you?"

"Please quit defending the man," Shannon snapped. "He's a liar and a swindler. I don't know how he managed to fool my grandmother into trusting him, but he doesn't fool me."

Coleen squared her shoulders. "Well, I still believe he's a good guy. He might be trying to save you from Barbara and her greedy family. It's clear she's behind all of this, don't you think?"

"I don't know what to think anymore. What I do know is we must find the necklace before someone else manages to get their hands on it."

"Do you have any ideas on where to start?"

"I've been thinking about the first line of the blessing on the needlepoint Victoria made, 'Blessing on a New Home'. There's a cross over the front door of this house. Would that be considered a blessing?"

Coleen jumped to her feet. "Och! Let's go and see."

"Hold on," Shannon said, frowning. "If we start snooping around the house, there's no way we'll be able to keep what we're doing from Deborah. She watches everything that goes on around here like a hawk."

Frustrated, Coleen collapsed back into the chair. "Well, what do you suggest we do?"

Shannon took a deep breath. "I wasn't certain at first, but I think I need to tell Deborah. She could be a big help in this, and I truly believe she can be trusted, don't you?"

"Yes, I do," Coleen reassured. "She's been faithful to your grandmother for so many years."

"I'm glad you agree. Now I have the rest of the day to try and figure this out. Tomorrow I need to start spending longer hours at the store, so I'll only have the evening to search. With any luck, we'll find it today."

Both women rose to their feet as one, eager to get started. They hurried downstairs to the front entrance to study the cross above the door.

"A blessing upon your new home." Shannon repeated the verse. She looked around for something to stand on.

"Here." Coleen lifted an empty flowerpot and turned it upside down.

Shannon stepped on it with one foot, but couldn't quite reach, so she raised herself up onto her tippy-toes. With the extra height, she barely reached the cross. She grasped it tight and pulled it down.

Coleen put the pot back, then looked around to make sure they weren't being watched. "C'mon."

They hurried over to a stone bench in the shade to examine the cross. It had been hand-carved from sandstone in a Celtic design. They turned it over, but could find no helpful markings or messages on it.

"Nothing." Coleen clucked her tongue.

"There must be something." Shannon turned the cross onto one side and then to the other.

"We could be wrong. Maybe the message isn't on the cross," Coleen suggested.

Shannon turned the cross upside down. "Or maybe it's inside it."

On the bottom of the cross she spotted a small hole, sealed with a piece of cork.

Excited, Coleen urged, "Let's have a look."

Shannon pulled the cork out. Inside she saw a piece of paper that had been rolled tight and inserted into the hole. She pulled it out and unfurled it.

She read aloud: "Not all hearths are new. Some tales are told in the flue."

Coleen tapped the side of her head with her palm. "Not another riddle."

Shannon grabbed her arm and pulled her up. "I believe I understand this one. But we'll have to talk to Deborah first. I need to find out which fireplace in this house is the newest."

They found Deborah in the kitchen, whipping up a dessert to go along with the dinner she'd already prepped.

"There you girls are." She stepped back to look them over. "You both have a nice glow from the sun."

"Could I speak to you for a minute?" Shannon asked.

Deborah's face fell, a look of fear upon it. "You're not going to can me, are you?"

"No, no, nothing like that. It's something else, something I need your help with."

Deborah leaned back against the counter and wiped her brow with her apron. "Good. You scared me there for a minute."

A security technician walked into the kitchen and started to pack up some equipment. "Do you mind if we go into your bedroom to talk?" Shannon asked quietly.

"Not at all."

They walked down a short hall, past the kitchen to Deborah's room. Her "room" was actually a bedroom with a queen-sized bed, with a separate bath off to the side, separated from the living area by a door. A couch, two easy chairs, a coffee table, and a television took up most of the living room. Through the window, Shannon could see a view of the shaded landscape on the east side of the house.

"Have a seat," Deborah offered.

Shannon and Deborah sat on the couch, and Coleen took an easy chair. Shannon handed Deborah the letter. "This came to me from Victoria's attorney. Read it."

They kept silent while she read. When finished, Deborah folded the letter slowly and handed it back to Shannon.

"It's so nice to see her handwriting." She sniffed back a few tears, then pulled a tissue from her pocket and blew her nose. "Reminds me of how much I miss her. She was such a good friend to me."

Shannon placed her hand over Deborah's. "I've taken you into my confidence based on that friendship."

The housekeeper matched Shannon's serious expression. "And you shall have it."

She shifted position on the couch. "Now, what do you want me to do?"

"We've found one clue." Shannon handed her the slip of paper they'd found in the cross. "Tell me, which of the fireplaces in this house is the newest?"

Deborah stared ahead, deep in thought. "I don't know. As far as I can remember, the fireplaces are all original to the house—but then I wasn't around when it was first built. Let me think."

A moment later, she jumped to her feet. "I've got it!"

"What's 'it'?" Coleen asked.

"The blue delft room, the one you're in, Coleen. The fireplace in that room was remodeled about five years ago. Victoria wanted it to match her blue-and-white theme. The Dutch tile on the fireplace is the new façade. The whole thing used to be stone. She ordered the tiles special from Holland, all handmade. What's the word? *Harlinger*—that's 'handmade' in Dutch."

"Let's go."

The three raced out of the room, but once they reached the kitchen, Deborah came to an abrupt stop. "What about my soufflé?"

Shannon leaned over and turned off the oven. "Shut off the chocolate on the double broiler. We'll eat later."

Deborah pulled off her apron and threw it onto a counter.

Her mouth widened in a big grin. "Okey-dokey."

They rushed upstairs to Coleen's room and began to examine the hearth. The fireplace was carved of white alabaster and inset with blue-and-white Dutch tiles depicting elements related to the sea: spiral shells, hermit crabs, mermaids, a starfish, lighthouse, and a seahorse.

"How could I have slept here and not even noticed how beautiful these tiles are?" Coleen shook her head.

Deborah tsk-tsked. "How could I have lived here for so many years and not appreciated them?"

"There's so much beauty in this house, it's hard not to take it for granted," Shannon said.

They examined the length of the fireplace, running their hands along the mantel and all around, looking for a hole similar to the one they'd found in the cross, but after ten minutes of searching, they'd found nothing.

Deborah ran her hands along the mantel's underside and came up with soot. "Ugh. Now that I'm properly soiled, you should ask me to look for anything else in this direction."

Shannon grabbed her arm and repeated the clue to her. "'Not all hearths are new. Some tales are told in the flue.' Of course, it must be hidden in the flue. Can you reach it?"

Excited, Deborah bobbed her head. She reached into the fireplace, and felt for the flue. "I have my hand on it."

"On the clue?" Shannon asked.

"No, the flue."

"The clue's in the flue ... who knew?" Coleen quipped.

"It's closed. I don't feel any air coming through. Should I open it?"

Shannon stroked her chin in thought. "Yes, there could be something on the other side."

Deborah pulled the handle on the flue. At once they felt a rush of air blow into the room. "My hands are filthy, for sure," she said. "I'll need coal tar soap to get all this soot off."

"Never mind about that," Coleen encouraged. "It will be worth it to find the necklace."

Head and shoulders against the blue tiles, Deborah extended her arm into the flue as she probed around. "There's nothing inside of the flue."

Disappointed, Shannon asked, "Did you feel the other side of the flue cover or whatever it's called?"

The strain of the awkward position started to show on Deborah's face. She grunted. "Doing it now … aha!"

"What is it?" Shannon and Coleen asked in unison.

Deborah pulled out a little metal box. Her hands blackened with soot, she turned it over. The bottom of the box was magnetized.

"Should we go downstairs to the kitchen?" Deborah suggested. "I think it would be easier to clean up if I opened this in the sink."

"Good thinking."

Deborah held the box far out in front of her as she walked, as if it contained an explosive device. Once in the kitchen, she placed it in the large stainless steel sink and opened it. Inside lay a piece of paper, folded into quarters.

Shannon carefully unfolded the paper.

"'Look for a sign,'" she read. "I think I understand this one."

"Well, what are you waiting for?" Coleen urged. "Lead the way."

Shannon shook her head. "Unfortunately, it will have to wait until morning. If my hunch is correct, the next clue is in the lake."

18

Early the next morning, the three women met in the kitchen. Shannon had brought the needlepoint with her. She surveyed the grounds through the window. "Just in case someone is watching the house, I believe I should go to the lake by myself. I'll make it look as if I'm taking a stroll, enjoying the morning air."

"Do you think we're under surveillance?" Deborah asked, eyes wide.

"I think it's possible." Shannon looked around the kitchen. "Do you have any coffee made?"

"Not yet, but give me a minute."

Shannon shook her head. "Give me a cup and saucer. I'll act my way through it."

Cup and saucer in hand, she exited through the back door and sauntered down the garden path to the point where it forked. She followed the path that led to the patio area with Adirondack chairs and took a seat, pretending all the while to sip from her empty cup.

After a time, she got up and continued her leisurely stroll, turning on the path to the lake, as if admiring the lily pads and the surrounding scenery. With casual nonchalance, she walked around to the place where she'd seen the strange sign in the tall grass near the edge of the lake.

She placed the cup and saucer on the ground, then

reached over and plucked the sign up out of the mud. Immediately, she noticed a small plastic bag, secured to the stick with string below the sign. She untied the string, grasped the bag, and quickly replaced the sign in the grass at the edge of the water.

With cup and saucer in hand again and the plastic package in her robe pocket, she wandered back to the kitchen, stopping to ponder the beauty of a flower and skim a smooth stone across the lake.

Back in the kitchen, Coleen and Deborah watched and waited, their cups filled with real coffee.

Shannon breezed in and held out her cup for Deborah to fill. "I could sure use some of that."

Coffee pot poised, Deborah asked, "Well?"

Shannon pulled the tiny package from her robe and opened the bag. Inside was a tiny picture frame.

"That's it?" Coleen moaned.

Shannon held up the frame to examine it. "No picture or note."

Coleen picked up the needlepoint from the kitchen table and read the verse: "'A blessing upon your spouse.'"

Shannon took a long sip of coffee and stared.

Deborah set the coffee pot down and snapped her fingers. "The painting of James in the hallway upstairs—could that be it? Unless of course she means *your* late husband. I wonder if she meant your spouse or hers? Oh, Victoria! This is all so like your grandmother."

Shannon put down her cup. "There's only one way to find out."

The three women bolted up the stairs.

The painting of James depicted him in uniform, a true captain of the sea, with piercing eyes the color of green agate, straight blond hair and a pointed beard.

"He must have been young when this was painted." Shannon observed.

Deborah stood back to admire it. "He never posed for it. Victoria had it painted after his death, from a picture. He was quite an attractive man, don't you think?"

"Yes," Shannon beamed. "He was. Once I get settled in, I intend to learn all that I can about my ancestors on his side of the family too."

Deborah opened her mouth to say something, but changed her mind.

Shannon felt along the back of the painting and discovered a clue taped to it.

"'Twin blessings,'" Shannon read aloud.

"That's easy," said Coleen. "Alec and Lara."

Shannon read the corresponding verse on the needlepoint. "'A blessing upon your growing son, upon your growing daughter.'"

"The pictures on Victoria's bedroom wall," Deborah said, quickly adding, "now *your* bedroom wall."

They hurried to the bedroom. Among the pictures of Shannon in the last row was a photograph of the twins when they were young.

Coleen found the two-word clue behind it. "'Deborah's room.'"

Shannon read the verse from the needlepoint: "'A blessing upon the household's helpers.'"

"I saw a similar needlepoint to this one on the wall in

Deborah's room," Coleen said. "Do you think Victoria would have hidden a clue there?"

Deborah raised her brows. "I suppose it's possible."

With their energy starting to wane, they walked at a more leisurely pace down the stairs and on to Deborah's room. Coleen spotted the needlepoint and lifted it off the wall.

"There's nothing here. I don't know how much more of this I can take," Coleen groaned. "The suspense is killing me."

Deborah shook her head. "We were doing so well. How could it not be there? Maybe the clue fell off."

"Or maybe we need to look for something else," Shannon reasoned.

"Whatever the answer, I say it's got to be somewhere in this room," Coleen said.

Shannon glanced at the clock on the wall with dismay. "I need to get cleaned up and head to the store. I've got to start a thorough inventory and get working on a business plan."

"If you'd like,I'll come with you," Coleen offered. "I can help you count and do anything else that needs to be done."

"That would be wonderful." Shannon looked around the room one last time. "I'm so disappointed. I thought surely we'd have found the necklace by now."

Deborah laid a hand on Shannon's shoulder. "Don't despair. Your grandmother was clever, but it's clear from her letter that she *did* want you to find it. And you will."

* * *

Later that evening, after a busy day at the store, Shannon and Coleen returned to the mansion, ready to continue their search.

"Dinner first?" Coleen hinted. "We can strategize."

"Of course."

They heated up Deborah's beef stroganoff and enjoyed it with a salad of baby greens, yellow tomatoes, and cucumbers. Dessert was caramel custard.

Coleen shoved a large spoonful of custard in her mouth and repeated the next verse on their list.

"*Wisth pawents*," She tilted her head to the side, deep in thought.

"What was that?" Shannon chuckled. "Are you trying to say 'wise parents'?"

Coleen squinted, and waved her empty spoon in the air for emphasis. "*Yeth.*" She swallowed. "Yum. Deborah is a jewel of a woman. Could I borrow her for a week or two?"

"I don't think I could part with her now. She has me spoiled already. If we don't find the necklace, I'm resolved to get a part-time job on top of my job at the store just so I can afford to keep her."

"Then I guess I'll have to visit often."

"I'll hold you to that." Shannon pulled out a pad of paper and a pencil. "Now, any ideas about the 'wise parents' verse? Wait, why are we jumping ahead to that one when we haven't solved the clue in Deborah's room yet?"

Coleen shrugged. "I thought we should move ahead."

"But we can't until we solve Deborah's. We need that clue to point us in the right direction."

"OK, but if that's the case, we're still stuck."

"Let's go back to her room and look around," Shannon said. "Maybe we'll get an idea. I don't think she'll mind if we poke around while she's out."

After they finished their meal, the two women returned to Deborah's room. While her friend scrutinized an Indian doll collection in a glass case, Shannon searched around the room. "Look at that sign, under the clock on the wall."

She pointed, and Coleen's eyes followed.

"'Bless this house?'"

"I recognize the letters. The sign on my grandmother's office at the store is painted in the same style. I can't believe I didn't notice it before."

Shannon pulled it off the wall. On the back, she found something written in longhand. "'Prov. 24: 3–4.'" She smiled and put the board back in place. "I think I know where to look. Follow me to my room."

Once in the room, Shannon went to the side table beside the bed and pulled her grandmother's Bible from the drawer. "The reference is to Proverbs, chapter 24, verses 3 and 4."

She leafed through the pages and stopped at the scripture.

"Proverbs 24:3–4: *'By wisdom a house is built, and through understanding it is established; through knowledge its rooms are filled with rare and beautiful treasures.*'"

"That scripture certainly describes the Paisley mansion," Coleen said. "'Its rooms are filled with rare and beautiful treasures.'"

"I agree."

Coleen brought her hands together. "What is that, written in the margin?"

Shannon drew closer, squinting. "It says, 'in my study, the unfinished work of my hands.'"

She put the Bible back in the drawer, and they hurried downstairs to the study. Shannon went straight to the painting. "That one was too easy. The cloth cover on the oil painting is a dead giveaway it's not finished."

She threw back the cloth to reveal a long road surrounded by dark trees. It was set at dusk, the mere hint of sun still in the sky, the road ahead foreboding.

Coleen shuddered. "I can't say I'm a fan of this one."

"It's not a pleasant painting, but it does rouse emotion." Shannon studied it. "Fear, mainly. But perhaps because I've had reason to fear lately."

Coleen came close and bent down to lean her head on Shannon's shoulder. "So true."

"Look, there." Shannon's finger traced along the winding road from top to bottom and ended at the signature. Instead of the expected "Victoria Paisley," the signature read, "Ledger." She reached for the needlepoint and read the next verse: "'Your goods and your income.'"

"That's appropriate," Coleen said.

"Ledger?" Shannon exchanged a confused glance with her friend. "All I can think of is one of those Charles Dickens-type of ledgers."

"Do you think your grandmother used one of those instead of a computer program?"

"You want the ledger?" Deborah asked from the doorway, startling them both. "It's in the drawer." She walked to a little wooden file cabinet under the worktable, opened it, and pulled out a thick tan ledger. Worn around the edges, it appeared to be ancient.

"How old is this?" Shannon asked.

"Got me," Deborah said. "But Victoria used it for as long as I knew her. Is that where the next clue is?"

Shannon nodded.

"Then I got back just in time."

Shannon opened the massive ledger and whisked the pages to the most recent entry. Again, it was written in her grandmother's hand, with fanciful flourishes. Shannon read it aloud: "'Summer house door.'"

Coleen picked up the needlepoint. "And the next line on this reads, 'A blessing upon kith and kin.'"

"What's that?" Deborah asked.

"Your native land and people," Coleen answered. "In our case, it's Scotland."

Shannon clasped her hands. "*Mìle fàilte.* We need to look around the summer house door. Deborah, do you know where there is a flashlight we could use?"

"Sure do. Be right back."

"We'll attract attention if someone is watching us." Coleen warned.

Shannon chewed her lip. "We're almost at the end. I won't be able to sleep if we don't take a look at that door tonight."

The path to the summer house was bathed in deep shadows, the crickets already in song. The women walked single file, Shannon in front, Coleen in the middle and Deborah at the end.

Shannon aimed the flashlight on the door and spotlighted the phrase "*Mìle fàilte.*" At the end of it she saw a small hinge. "Did you ever notice this before, Deborah?"

Deborah stepped in closer for a better look. "No, and I must have looked at this door a million times. I guess we only see what we're prepared to see."

"Coleen, can you lift the hinge while I keep the light on it?"

"Sure." Lifting the hinge revealed a cutout in the wood of the thick door. Inside it they found a silver and mother-of-pearl baby teething ring, and a note.

Coleen handed the items to Shannon. She shone the flashlight on the note. "*E.A.P.*"

"Whose initials?" Coleen asked.

"My mother's," Shannon said. "Elizabeth Ann Paisley."

Deborah held the needlepoint. Both women turned to her for the verse.

"'A blessing upon children yet unborn.'" Her eyes narrowed for a moment. "Could Victoria's clue be somehow related to the nursery? It's actually Beth's old room. 'Course it doesn't look like a nursery anymore. It changed through the years from a nursery to a little girl's room to a teen girl's room and then ..."

Shannon dropped the teething ring into her pocket. "Lead the way."

Back in the house, they climbed two flights of stairs and headed down a long hall toward the back of the house.

"Who needs a gym membership in a house like this?" Coleen panted.

Deborah opened the door at the end of the hall and flipped on the light. "This was Beth's room."

The window and balcony faced the rear of the house.

With the gardens and lake to look at, Shannon imagined the view would have been wonderful. She'd peeked in the room for a brief look during the initial tour, but she hadn't had time to properly explore it. Now, knowing it to be the room her mother grew up in, it seemed even more special.

A white wrought iron bed set near the French doors was piled high with fluffy down pillows and a white chenille bedspread. Collectible dolls in special cases lined one whole shelf along the east wall, and a collection of cameras were grouped on the shelf beneath it.

Shannon reached for a picture on a kidney-shaped dressing table. "My mother was beautiful."

"Yes, she was." Deborah said. "Victoria never redecorated this room. She told me that after Beth went off to college, she sometimes would come in here and hug a teddy bear and cry herself to sleep. Isn't that sad?"

"It's heartbreaking," Coleen said. "But any mother can relate."

Shannon steeled her heart against the empathy that threatened to form. She refused to feel any emotion for her grandmother. Not after what she'd done to her own daughter.

"What are we looking for in here?" Deborah asked.

"I'm not sure. Another baby item, perhaps?"

"Or ..." Coleen pointed to a cross-stitch sampler on the wall that bore the initials E.A.P. "Perhaps our next clue is hidden in that?"

"Good thinking." Shannon pulled it off the wall. "There's a note taped to the back. It says, 'Life isn't always black and white.'"

"What's the next verse, Deborah?" Coleen glanced

around the room, ready to pounce. "With any luck, the necklace will be in here."

"'A blessing in light or darkness.'"

Coleen groaned. "I don't understand that. Do either of you?"

Bent over, Deborah studied a bulletin board filled with photographs. As she straightened up, both Coleen and Shannon saw her wince. She pointed to a picture in the center of the bulletin board. Voice strained, she announced, "This might be it."

Shannon joined her. "Does your back hurt?"

"Don't mind me," Deborah said. "It acts up now and then."

"Why don't you sit down? That might help."

Deborah lowered herself into a chair.

Shannon studied the photograph, the only one on the board in black and white. "It's a picture of my mother, and she's taking a picture."

"Your mother's favorite childhood hobby was photography."

Shannon looked around the room. "Of course. The pictures, the shelf full of vintage cameras ..."

Coleen jumped off the edge of the bed to look at the cameras. She let out a little whimper. Her hand shook as she pulled a note from a Hasselblad and read, "'Secrets will always be exposed.'"

Deborah shrugged. "I have no idea."

Coleen made a face. "For someone who was reported to be deathly ill during her last days, your grandmother has sure managed to send us on a dead-end goose chase."

Shannon plopped down onto the bed and buried her

head in a pillow. She was exhausted after the long day, and fresh out of ideas. What she needed was a good night's sleep.

Deborah had invited them to attend church with her at the early service the next morning. The timing was perfect. Shannon was fairly certain it was going to take a miracle to find the necklace.

— 19 —

On Monday morning, Coleen and Shannon hurried to the back of the craft store to join their new friends. Melanie had called a special meeting of the Purls, and they were both anxious to find out why.

Melanie's marionberry muffins and a thermal jug of chai tea sat in the middle of the table with an assortment of mugs. The baskets were already in front of each of the chairs, even one for Coleen. The women began to knit right away. They caught up on each other's lives, and talked about everything from pets, to raising children, to the state of the economy.

Though they'd managed to squeeze in another chair for Coleen, the whole area was a bit tight for Shannon's taste. "You know, we, meaning Coleen and I, have been thinking about ways to streamline the inventory and make better use of space in the shop. If I do that, maybe we could make this area a little bigger."

Betty looked at the others before replying. "Why Shannon, it's so interesting you would bring that up. Victoria had the same idea. Her dream was to expand this area into a special room. She planned to add a coffee shop and an area where craft groups dedicated to raising money for charities could meet."

"She even had an architect draw up plans and get the

permits," Joyce added. "But then she got sick, and the project fell to the wayside."

"Where are those plans?" Shannon asked.

Betty looked to the others. "Maybe at your house? Or if they're here, maybe Morgan knows where they are. I'm sure you could find out who the architect was."

"Thank you. I'll check into it." Shannon envisioned the wall behind them knocked out and a room filled with windows beyond. In her mind's eye, she pictured a coffee barista behind a counter laden with pastries and teas, a collection of comfortable easy chairs, and a place for charity items to be offered for sale.

The other women focused on their knitting, engrossed in counting stitches. But Shannon had learned long ago how to knit without thinking, as if she had a calculator in one part of her brain that counted every stitch. She looked around the room and her gaze settled on Melanie.

It struck her how good Melanie looked compared to their last meeting. Today, a warm pink glow brightened her face. "Melanie, you look wonderful," she observed. "What's your secret?"

Melanie bit her lip. "Do I?" A sly smile crept across her face.

"Yes, do tell us your secret," Joyce said. "And how long are you going to keep us in suspense about your big news? I'm dying to know."

"I'll kill two birds with one stone." Melanie clasped her hands. "My secret is simple. It's a clean bill of health from my doctor."

The women all screamed in unison.

Melanie continued. "When I found out yesterday, I felt like I had a new lease on life. I went shopping and bought new clothes, and new makeup too. I ate cookies for lunch and took in a double feature at the movie theater."

Shannon smiled. "I'm so happy for you."

"What about you?" Melanie asked. "How are you adjusting to your new home?"

Shannon told her new friends about the break-in and caught them up on her one-on-one silversmith classes with Harold Giddings. She and Coleen talked about the beach. And of course, Coleen talked about Michael. As Coleen talked, Shannon caught her wink and twitch her face in her direction, clearly trying to get the other women on board with her matchmaking plans.

As a result, Shannon spent the next ten minutes assuring the group she was *not* at all interested in a relationship right now, especially with Michael Stone. However, she did not go into detail as to why.

Then Betty asked the question Shannon dreaded: "What time are you taking Coleen to the airport next Saturday?"

"Nine o'clock," Shannon answered. "In the morning."

"How would you like a little friendly company? I know it's going to be a hard day for you. We could grab lunch on the way home."

"Oh, Betty, that's very nice of you. Are you sure? It's so far."

"Don't be silly. It's less than an hour away."

Kate spoke up. "I'll come too. I could use a day off."

Joyce threw her hands into the air. "Hold on, did I just hear you say you're actually taking a day off? You *never* do that."

Kate lifted her nose. "Well, I'm going to. In fact, I've decided I'm going to take a day off every week. I can't continue at the pace I've been going."

The ladies began a spontaneous fit of cheering. "Good for you!"

"Save room for me," Melanie said. "I'm coming too."

"Uh-oh," Shannon said. "Unless you all want to sit in the back of a very old and smelly truck, I won't have enough room for everyone."

"You're referring to that Jurassic blue creature Victoria would never part with?" Betty asked. "I've got a better idea. I'll drive."

"Oh, thank goodness!" Joyce laughed so hard, she snorted.

The room erupted into laughter.

Later, after the meeting concluded, Betty approached Shannon with an idea. The Purls wanted to throw a going-away party for Coleen on her last night in Apple Grove. Whispering so Coleen wouldn't overhear, they decided the Paisley mansion would be the best location. Joyce had already volunteered to bring the cake, so Shannon agreed to ask Deborah to prepare a special meal.

After the women left, Shannon brought her collection of beads, antique findings, and other materials with her to the front desk. While Morgan and a part-time employee continued with the store inventory—under Coleen's eagle eye—she'd decided to set up camp and bead a few examples for the lighted display cases she and Coleen had found in the stockroom while cleaning and organizing. She planned to bead some real showstoppers with the cache of Vendome and Regency beads, and some rondells she'd come across.

Deciding on a Regency-inspired necklace in a *coquelicot* color palette of saturated poppy with hints of pink and orange, she chose beads made of pink-orange corundum, hyacinth crystal, and Indian red Swarovski crystal beads. The closure would be a fish hook clasp and an extension link chain with a metal ball at the end.

Shannon set out all the beads, spacers, and tiger wire she would need, as well as her tools. Then she got to work.

A short while later, the bell above the door tinkled. Shannon looked up to see a young woman with shiny coils of caramel and chocolate brown hair enter the shop. Dressed in a long skirt, hand-woven belt, and linen tank top, she smiled and approached the desk.

As she extended her hand, the jingle of bangle bracelets accented her movements. "Hi. I'm Essie Engleman."

Taking the girl's hand, Shannon shook it and introduced herself. "Shannon McClain."

"I'm not here to shop."

Shannon eyed her. "Oh?"

"Are you the manager?"

"I'm the owner. The manager is busy."

"Even better. Do you need any help right now? I'm looking for full-time employment, but I'd be happy to take any job that'll keep my lights on."

"What kind of full-time job are you looking for?"

Essie bit her bottom lip. "I don't think you'd be interested since you already have a manager."

"I take it you have management experience?"

"I grew up working in the family drugstore in Florida. I know how to take inventory, stock shelves, work the registers, and help the pharmacist, though I don't guess you'd be needing that last skill."

"Do you craft?"

"Do I craft? Crafting and art is what I live for." Essie noticed the beads on the desk and her eyes lit up. "And I *love* beading."

"Really?"

Essie lifted up the set of beads around her own neck. "I made it."

Shannon admired the novelty of the piece. Composed of several antique brooches and beads in a citron as pale as the inner rind of a lemon, it had an old-world feel to it. "Very nice."

"It's just one of my many creations."

Shannon looked the girl over. She seemed pleasant enough. And a new manager would soon be in order. "Do you have a résumé?"

"Who's this?" Morgan interrupted them as she fanned through pages on the clipboard in her hand.

Shannon reached for the résumé Essie handed to her. "Essie. She's here to apply for a job."

Without making eye contact, Morgan wrote something on the clipboard and muttered, "We have all the help we need. Come back some other time."

Essie nodded and turned to go.

"Wait, don't leave." Shannon glanced at Morgan, then back at the girl. "I consider myself a good judge of people. You're hired."

Essie's face lit up and she clasped her hands together. "I am?"

"You can start right now by helping us with inventory." Shannon turned to Morgan and met her icy stare steadily. "Please show her what to do."

Morgan's face contorted into a nasty sneer. "You think you're so smart, don't you? Think you've got it all figured out. Well, you don't. And you're in for a nasty surprise. I only wish I could be here to see your face when your little world comes crashing down around you. But I'm sick of putting up with your foolishness. I quit. Good luck trying to run this business without me." She threw down her clipboard, grabbed her purse from behind the desk, and stormed out the door.

Essie's mouth formed a perfect O. But in the awkward silence that followed, Shannon realized the room felt lighter, as if a dark cloud that hung over the place had finally lifted. Though it was sad to think of Morgan as a malevolent cloud, the woman did have a nasty disposition—and she'd never produced the requested list of items that had been sold since Victoria's death. Shannon was glad to be rid of her.

Shannon cleared her throat. "I apologize for that. Getting back to your résumé ..." She took a closer look at it. "Hmmm, a degree in microbiology? And a master's as well? With your educational background and awards, why do you want to do this kind of work?"

"My parents wanted me to major in the sciences. To be honest, I sailed through all of my courses in science, math, and physics. But I never enjoyed any of it."

"Why not?"

Essie shrugged. "I'm an artist at heart. That's all I've ever wanted to be. But my parents didn't see a future in it, and they discouraged me from majoring in art. The truth is, they refused to pay for it."

"What do you do now?"

"I paint, craft, and sell my art. I've been trying to find full-time work. I'm anxious to settle somewhere. I'm tired of traveling, but I don't want to work in an office or anything like that. It's important to me that I love what I do." Her eyes twinkled. "I have some other unique talents as well."

Amused, Shannon asked, "Such as?"

"I design 3-D images and paint them in sidewalk chalk. They're pretty cool. People seem to like them."

"Oh, yes, I've seen those before." Shannon told her about the goldfish pond and some of the other designs she'd seen in Portland near the food trucks.

Essie flashed a smile. "That was most likely me. I live in Portland now."

"I love it. It's truly amazing what you can do."

Essie took a bow. "Thank you."

Shannon thought for a moment. "In addition to the store, I also have an online business, and I'll need someone to oversee it. Are you Web-savvy?"

"I'm good with computers. I'd have no problem processing orders."

"Good." Shannon folded the résumé in half. "What do your parents think of what you're doing now?"

Essie played with the bangles on her wrist. "They think I'm throwing my life away."

"I disagree." Shannon extended her hand. "Welcome to the Paisley Craft Market & Artist Lofts. As luck would have it, we've just had a new position open up. How would you like to be my new manager?"

— 20 —

Saturday morning came faster than either Shannon or Coleen wanted it to. After a week of searching, they still hadn't found the necklace, and Coleen was sick about having to leave before the mystery was solved.

Betty and the ladies picked them up in Betty's SUV, and they set out for the Portland airport. Though the conversation was light and fun during the drive, by the time they reached the airport, the mood had taken a somber turn. The six of them stuck close together as they walked through the terminal. When they reached the security area, the Purls showered Coleen with hugs and good wishes. Then they found a bench to sit on nearby while Shannon said a private goodbye to her dear friend.

Near the security entrance, Coleen took off her pumps and held them in her hands. "Well, my friend, this is it. What a lonely flight it will be without you by my side."

"I'm confident you'll meet new people on the plane." Shannon focused her gaze upward. "As soon as you fall asleep and start calling the geese, you'll be the center of attention, I'm sure."

Coleen giggled. "I can still picture the look on that man's face from the flight over. A pill for snoring—who's ever heard of such a thing?"

Shannon handed her a black box tied with a bow

of bright pink ribbon.

Coleen held it in her right hand. "What's this?"

"Just a little something to make sure you won't forget me."

"Like *that* could ever happen." Coleen tugged at the ribbon and it fell away. She lifted the cover off the box. Inside was Shannon's first silversmith creation, a cross with a brass heart in the center, buffed and polished to a high sheen.

Coleen gasped at the sight of it. Tears welled in her eyes as she held up the beaded necklace with the cross pendant. "You even used my favorite beads, the Italian glass ones I asked you for."

"Of course I did." Shannon embraced her. "You deserve the best."

"I love it. Thank you."

"Do you want to put it on?"

Coleen shook her head. "Not yet. I'm still admiring it."

"It's only my first attempt. The shaping could have been better, and I would've cut the heart at a better angle if—"

"Nonsense. It's perfect."

Her voice wavering, Shannon grabbed Coleen's hand. "This isn't really goodbye. I'll be back before you know it."

"Only to pack up your house and leave again," Coleen pouted. "I miss you already."

"I know the feeling." A sob rose in Shannon's throat, and she wrapped her arms one more time around her friend.

Coleen hugged her back and then attempted to disentangle herself from the embrace. "OK, I'd better get moving, or I'm going to miss my flight."

Reluctantly, Shannon let her go. She waved at Coleen

as she passed through security, and she continued to wave until her friend disappeared out of sight down the terminal. She choked back tears for a moment before she rejoined her new friends.

"Oh, honey." Betty took one look at Shannon and gave her a hug. "I know that had to hurt."

Kate patted her shoulder. "I hate saying goodbye too, except in the case of my old boyfriend. I *enjoyed* saying goodbye to him, but that was months ago. I'll tell you the story on the way back."

Joyce groaned. "We've heard it a million times."

"But Shannon hasn't," Kate argued. "And she needs to be caught up on these kinds of things."

Betty and Kate threaded their arms through Shannon's, and the Purls saw her home.

* * *

Shannon went straight to her room the moment she returned to the mansion. For the next few hours, she cried into her pillow, mourning the loss of her friend, her old life, and all that she called familiar. The feelings she could no longer escape began to bubble up.

All alone in a new place, a new life, and in a house full of secrets.

She stepped out onto the balcony and released her hair from its tidy chignon. The wind caught it, flipping it around in every direction. She sat down in her grandmother's chair and soaked in the sun for a while, trying to relax.

I should be back at work. Essie had assured her she was

ready to cover the floor and the store with the help of a part-timer. But Shannon couldn't help but worry. She decided to grab a cup of tea, and then head to the store.

She entered the kitchen as Deborah came in through the back door, a basket of flowers and vegetables in her hands. "There you are. I was just coming in to find you. You have a visitor waiting for you in the summer house."

"Who is it?" Shannon asked.

"I'm not at liberty to say." Deborah went to the sink and filled a vase with water. "I'll be leaving in a bit. I have to run to the grocery store."

"OK … I guess I'll go see who the mystery person is." Shannon's heart beat faster. Perhaps Coleen had changed her mind and decided to stay a little longer? She hurried down the path, quickening her steps until she reached the door of the summer house.

She threw it open. "Coleen! I knew—"

Her voice faltered at the sight of a strange woman. She stood with her back to the door, staring out at the lake. When Shannon approached, the woman turned to face her.

"I recognize you," Shannon said, perplexed. "You work at that food truck in Portland. What are you doing here?"

"I'm the woman whose baby picture is in the locket you're wearing."

Shannon grasped the locket and studied the woman's face. A wave of shock overcame her as she realized the woman was her mother. She looked much older than she had in any photograph Shannon had seen. But there was no mistaking the resemblance. "You really are … Beth?"

"I am."

"I can't believe this is happening." Shannon staggered backward a few steps and sank onto the couch. Beth sat down next to her. She tried to put an arm around Shannon's shoulders, but Shannon shrugged her away.

"Are you all right?" Beth asked.

"I'm in shock."

"I understand this is hard for you. It's hard for me too."

"I thought you were dead!" Shannon burst into tears.

Beth's voice trembled. "I know you must have a million questions. Could we stay here and talk for a while?"

Shannon gave her a faint nod. She felt drained, spent of emotion.

"You can ask me anything you want," Beth invited gently. She reached over to stroke her hair, but when she saw Shannon's pained expression, she withdrew her hand.

To Shannon, the moment was like a dream, the culmination of years of tears on her pillow, of hopes and prayers to be reunited with her mother. But now that her prayers had been answered, all she could manage to do was coil tightly within herself as she attempted to protect her heart from further damage and lies.

Hugging herself close, Shannon said, "Nadine told me you left us because you had a multiple personality disorder. She said Victoria locked you up in an institution, where you later died. Clearly that last part was a lie."

"*All* of it was a lie. Aunt Nadine has a long history of mental problems. She spent some time in an institution when she was young," Beth explained. "That was probably the inspiration for her story."

"Then how did she end up so wealthy, and living independently?"

"She was beautiful in her youth, and men were smitten with her. Many were more than willing to overlook her 'quirks.' She only married wealthy men. She's been widowed more than once, and she amassed a new fortune each time."

"Then what was your excuse for abandoning us?" Shannon's voice turned bitter.

"Although it must seem like I did abandon you from your perspective, I didn't. I left to protect you—and your father." Beth stood and began to pace. "In 1976, I was working for a wire service as a reporter. I'd written an article about a secretive criminal organization, the Camorra, who had ancient ties to Scotland and a handful of other countries. They were smuggling weapons to various terrorist organizations, including the IRA. Members of the Camorra learned about my article and threatened to kill me if it ever appeared in print."

"But you turned it in anyway?"

"I was young, undaunted, and stupid. The article ran, and it was picked up by hundreds of papers. Soon afterward, I learned the Camorra planned to take not only my life, but yours and your father's. The police could offer us no real help or protection. A few of them were corrupt as well."

Shannon regarded her with disgust. "So you ran off and left Dad and me there to be killed?"

"There's more to the story. We have roots in Scotland. A family member offered to negotiate our safety for a price, so Victoria did what any mother would do. She engaged him to broker a deal with the Camorra."

"My Great-Uncle Trevor?" Things were beginning to fall into place in Shannon's mind.

"That's right. He brokered the deal. The Camorra agreed to it, but only with a certain stipulation."

"They forced you to leave?"

Beth nodded. "I had to leave Scotland in exchange for your lives. They warned me that if I tried to take you or your father with me, they'd find us all and make good on their threat. I didn't want to risk it."

Shannon felt some of her anger toward her mother melt away. "Is that all?"

"They also demanded money, of course. They knew my mother was wealthy. They extorted money from her for years, through Trevor."

Suddenly alarmed, Shannon thought of the twins. "Are they still demanding payment? There's not much cash left in the estate ..."

"No. Trevor has been pocketing all of the money for himself for many years, I'm sure of it. I could never convince Mother of that though."

"If that's the case, why did you continue to stay away?" Shannon challenged.

"Because I was terrified—of this very moment. I wasn't sure if you'd understand ... or if you'd hate me for what I'd done."

Shannon didn't respond.

Beth sat down next to her again and searched her face. "I can't tell you how many nights I agonized over what I'd done. If only I hadn't taken the job, hadn't written the article, how our lives could've been different." She paused.

"Normal."

"I understand why you did it."

Beth squeezed Shannon's hand. "But that doesn't make it any better, does it? I wasn't there to dress your skinned knees or make your lunches, or see you go on your first date. I wasn't there to help you when Alec and Lara were born."

"No, you weren't."

"And I'm so sorry." Beth's voice caught. "I had to leave you and Spencer, and it was the hardest thing I've ever done. Sometimes ... sometimes in the dark years that followed, I thought it might have been better if I had just died."

In the silence that followed, Shannon drew her knees up to her chest. She looked into her mother's eyes, green as peridots. The face was so familiar, yet so distant; it was kind, but it showed more signs of sorrow than of sweetness.

"What have you been doing for the past thirty-six years?" Shannon asked.

"Oh, I've done a lot of different things. I drifted for a time, taking part-time jobs here and there. Now I own a Gourmet on the Go business in Portland."

"Did you keep in touch with Victoria?"

"Yes. We worked out a way to keep in contact, through people who could be trusted. That's how I kept up with you and your father."

"He hardly ever spoke of you. Sometimes I wondered if he hated you."

"We loved each other very much."

Shannon thought for a moment, allowing everything to sink in. "So Deborah must have known the truth all along?"

Beth nodded. "I asked her not to tell you anything. I

wanted to be the one to answer all of your questions. I've waited for so many years."

"Why did you come today?" Shannon narrowed her eyes; she couldn't help feeling suspicious. "Are you hoping to get part of Victoria's estate?"

Beth appeared genuinely hurt. "Not at all. My mother gave me a large sum of money many years ago to invest and live off of. I have all the money I need. I came today because of Deborah. She told me what Nadine said to you. I had to set the record straight. I'd already planned to come back and meet you. I've thought of nothing else since the day you showed up at my food truck. But I had to work up the nerve."

"Are you going to stay here tonight?"

"If you'll have me."

Shannon took a deep breath and slowly exhaled. "I'd like that."

On their way out the door, Shannon noticed the Gaelic greeting and thought about the letter. She spun around to face Beth. "Could you help me with something?"

"Of course, anything."

"Victoria left me a letter. In it she claims there's a valuable necklace hidden somewhere on the estate. She wanted me to have it as part of my inheritance. If I don't find it, I doubt I'll be able to keep the home or the business afloat for long. I wonder if you could help me decipher the last two clues. I haven't had any luck with them so far."

Beth nodded. "I'll certainly try. Mom was a master at creating and solving puzzles."

"The two clues are 'A blessing in light or darkness' and 'Secrets will always be exposed.'"

Beth thought a moment. "There's something about the words 'light,' 'darkness,' and 'exposed.' Perhaps she's referring to my old darkroom."

"There's a darkroom in the house?"

Beth nodded. "It's in the east turret."

"That must be it!" Shannon could hardly contain her excitement. It was the last of the clues. The necklace had to be somewhere in that room. "Let's go take a look."

They hurried down the path to the mansion, but the sound of a gun being cocked stopped both women in their tracks.

"Not so fast, ladies."

— 21 —

Shannon whirled to find Nadine standing on the path, an ivory-handled pistol in her hand.

Shannon took a step back.

"Don't move." The corners of Nadine's mouth turned up. "I see you've finally found your long-lost mother. How very touching."

"Liar. You said she was crazy." Shannon fought to control her anger. "And dead."

"What can I say?" Nadine shrugged and looked at Beth. "I was hoping you were."

Beth kicked at a little pebble in front of her. "It's really no surprise Nadine lied to you about the mental institution, Shannon. Your great-aunt has seen the inside of quite a few of them over the years. She knows all about them." She took a step forward.

Eye twitching, Nadine trained the pistol on Beth. "Stop right there."

Beth stopped and folded her arms. "You're one crazy old bat."

"How dare you talk to me like that!"

"My mother has a point," Shannon commented, picking up on Nadine's discomfort. Perhaps if they could unnerve the woman enough to divert her attention, one of them might be able to knock the pistol from her hand, or at least run away and get help. "After all, you *are* holding us at gunpoint."

Nadine shifted the focus of her gun toward Shannon. Then back to Beth.

Beth turned to Shannon so Nadine couldn't see her wink with her left eye. "There's no use in denying it," Beth continued. "You've had more than your fair share of mental problems over the years."

"That's enough!" Clearly agitated, the old woman waved her gun at them. "Put your hands up, both of you. And quit your fidgeting."

When they hesitated, she added, "I have no qualms about shooting either one of you. I'm insane, remember?"

Shannon and Beth exchanged glances and raised their arms.

Shannon's mouth felt dry and her heart hammered inside her chest. "What do you want?" she asked.

"How dimwitted *are* you? I want the necklace."

"I'm the only one who knows where it is," Beth said. Then she nodded in her daughter's direction. "Let her go, and I'll take you to it. You don't need her. You need me."

Shannon looked at Beth. It struck her hard when she realized that even though Beth was practically a stranger, she was still willing to make the ultimate sacrifice for her.

Nadine shook her head. "You must think I'm stupid."

"No one thinks you're stupid," Shannon said. "But you *are* deluded. You can't possibly believe you'll get away with this."

Nadine looked at Beth. "Tell the girl who she's dealing with. She clearly doesn't know me very well."

"What am I supposed to tell her? That you're good at conning rich men into marrying you and then making them kick the bucket before nature intended? I doubt she'd be impressed."

"You always did have a smart mouth. But you'll regret that remark." Face flushed, Nadine motioned with her gun. "Now start walking."

Beth kept a slow pace, dragging out the walk back to the kitchen. Shannon matched her every step.

"Deborah's probably called the police by now," Shannon warned. "She doesn't miss a thing."

Nadine let out a sinister laugh. "Oh, I highly doubt that."

Shannon spun around. "What did you do to her?"

"I haven't done anything to her—yet. But if you don't turn back around and start walking, who can say what might happen?"

The women progressed slowly toward the main house. As they approached the back door, Nadine ordered them to stop. With the gun still trained on the women, she pulled a two-way radio from her waistband and spoke into it. "Is the house secure?"

A man's voice answered. "Aye."

"Did you disable the security system like I told you to?"

"I did."

"Good. We're on our way in."

She waved the pistol at the women. "Get moving. And Beth, you start talking. Where is the necklace?"

Beth took a deep breath. "I believe it's in the east turret."

"You 'believe' it's there? Or you know for sure?"

"Victoria hid it," Shannon interjected. "She left riddles to solve that would lead me to it. I understood all of them, save for the final one. That is, until Beth showed up."

"My sister and her blasted riddles." Nadine stomped her foot. "She was nothing but an overgrown child. Now hurry up and get inside. I'm on a tight schedule."

The women entered the French doors leading to the kitchen. Inside, a man blocked their path. Short and smarmy-looking, his beady eyes chilled Shannon to the core. When he moved aside to allow them to pass, she noticed the cobra tattoo on his neck.

"It's you!" Shannon exclaimed.

"Aye. We meet again." He grinned, revealing grayish husks of teeth.

"You were the one lurking around my house, the man who tried to steal the package. And you left that note on my door too, didn't you?"

Nadine stepped next to him. "Snake doesn't need to answer your questions. He works for me. And he's done a fine job, mostly. How's your shoulder today, pet?"

Snake glared at Shannon as he lifted his shirt to reveal a thick bandage on his left shoulder.

"I think Snake's a little angry with you for stabbing him," Nadine taunted. "I can't blame him for feeling that way."

They heard a noise coming from the breakfast room. Without thinking, Shannon stepped forward to look around the corner.

"Stop right there," Nadine commanded.

But Shannon had gone far enough to see Deborah, seated

in a chair at the breakfast table. Her arms and legs were restrained by ropes, her mouth had been gagged, but she rocked the chair back and forth and issued muffled shouts. Her eyes met Shannon's. They were filled with anger, fear, and confusion. It was evident Deborah hadn't made it to the grocery store.

Happy to see her alive and well, Shannon mouthed the words "Don't worry" to her friend. Seeing the older woman in such a state broke her heart. She said a prayer under her breath. Whether by an act of heroism or divine intervention, Nadine had to be stopped.

Nadine's eyebrows drew together. "Now then, you girls are going to lead me to the necklace. If you don't, things are going to get ugly around here. Do you understand what I'm saying?"

Shannon nodded, fear crawling up her spine.

"As you wish," Beth answered evenly.

Nadine turned to Snake as they exited the room. "Check in with me periodically."

"Yes, ma'am." He leered at Shannon as she passed.

The women crossed the stone floor of the foyer, then Beth led them up the stairs and down a long hallway to her old room. Shannon could hear Nadine panting behind her after the climb, and for the first time in her life, she wished for someone to have a heart attack.

Beth opened the bedroom door and headed straight for the closet. A shoe rack mounted on a portion of the back wall held dozens of wrinkly shoes. Beth reached under a pair of vintage boots and turned a doorknob. When she pushed open the hidden door, a blast of chilled air hit them from the black hole of darkness beyond.

Shannon pretended to trip as she followed Beth through the secret door. She fell against the wall, sending hatboxes raining down on her.

Beth turned. "Are you all right?"

"Clumsy fool," Nadine muttered. "Never mind about her—get going."

But the ruse worked. Shannon had hoped to grab a high-heeled shoe, but the hatboxes offered something even better—a hatpin. She slid the long, decorative pin up her sleeve. *Now to find the right opportunity to use it.*

"There's a light switch somewhere on the wall." Beth reached in and began to feel for it. "Ah, here it is."

She flipped the switch numerous times to no avail. But as their eyes adjusted to the darkness, it became apparent the passageway was dimly lit by a natural light source as well. Even in the low light, the chains of dust that clung to the walls like vines were visible.

"This way." Beth crept forward. At the end of the short hall was a curved stairway.

"Oh, for goodness sake. Another flight of stairs? You'd better not be playing games," Nadine warned.

"I'm doing as you asked," Beth replied sharply. "I'm taking you to the place where I think the necklace is hidden."

"I can't imagine how my sister got up here to hide the thing," Nadine grumbled. "I always suspected she wasn't as sick as she pretended to be."

Caked with years of dust and grime, the rectangular windows along the stairway shed just enough light on their path. They stopped at a narrow door at the top of the stairs.

A faded "Keep Out" sign welcomed them.

Beth creaked the door open and stepped inside. When she pulled on a chain that hung from the ceiling, a single red bulb lit the small space. The circular room had rows of shelves. Shannon could just make out brown glass containers, photo paper, stainless steel thermometers, and other utensils.

The three women crowded around the counter and sink that occupied most of the space. Hanging from a clothesline above them, black-and-white photos presented a timeline of a happier, carefree life.

Shannon noticed a smiling portrait of Victoria, her hair done up in an elaborate style, diamond hairpins at her temples. Clearly a joyful woman, even in black and white, her eyes sparkled with life and vitality.

Shannon's eyes moved hungrily to the next photo—a photo of her mother. It showed a confident young woman leaning against a white picket fence. With flawless skin and long hair flowing in the breeze, she wore a smile that spoke of a life of nurture and ease—a polar opposite to the dark direction her life had taken.

Shannon glanced at her mother. Beth had a quiet strength about her, and the confidence was still there. The element that had changed in her countenance was sorrow. She'd known a life of sadness, of living in the shadows, of longing for her loved ones. Shannon tried to imagine what it must have been like for her.

The next photo was a mother-daughter composition. In spite of the situation, Shannon felt a smile bloom across her face as she reached out to touch it.

"Don't touch anything unless I tell you to," Nadine snapped. She brandished the gun again. "Beth, find that necklace. There's no time to waste. I have a flight to catch."

Beth began to search through boxes. As she did, Shannon took the opportunity to distract Nadine. "It must be awful for you, being so much in debt."

Nadine glared at her. "How would you know about that?"

"I put two and two together. You wouldn't be going to such desperate measures if you didn't need it; $350,000 is a good chunk of money, but it's no fortune by your standards."

The woman glanced at her watch. "You're right about that."

"It seems to me you're good at acquiring money, but not so good at keeping it. What was it? Bad investments? Too many Cadillacs?"

"I don't like your tone," Nadine snarled. "If you must know, recent events in the stock market wiped me out. I need the money from the necklace to start over."

"It's not going to work."

"That's where you're wrong, my dear. I've been in this situation before, and I always land on my feet." Her gaze drifted off. "Always."

Beth knocked a bottle off a shelf and it shattered on the floor.

"Stupid woman!" Nadine yelled. "Haven't you found it yet?"

"It's not in any of the boxes," Beth answered. "I'm going to check in the cabinets underneath."

"Be quick about it. How hard can it be to find one little

necklace?" Nadine gestured to Shannon. "Go help her."

"I thought you didn't want me to touch anything."

"Don't get snide with me." She leveled the pistol at Shannon's head.

Shannon crouched and opened a cabinet. She began to rifle through it, finding more photo paper, clips, an apron, white cotton gloves, and a container of talc, which seemed out of place.

As she pulled things out of the cabinets, the mess grew wider on the terrazzo-tiled floor. Leaning her elbow back on the floor to steady herself, she encountered a loose tile. Shannon looked up. The red bulb hung directly above the loose tile. She repeated the clue in her head: "*A blessing in light or darkness ... secrets will always be exposed.*" Could the necklace be under the tile? And if they gave Nadine what she wanted now, what would happen to them?

She might kill us both.

Shannon ran her fingers up her sleeve and felt the hat-pin. If she could surprise Nadine, perhaps catch her off guard, then maybe they could get the upper hand. She glanced back at the woman.

But Nadine was alert and watching them like a hawk. Surprising her wouldn't be easy.

As Shannon continued to pull things out of the cabinet, she formulated a plan. *The talcum powder.* In one swift movement, she grabbed it and jumped from her crouching position to squeeze the bottle at Nadine's face.

The gun exploded, and Shannon felt the bullet sail past her ear. She lunged at the old woman, struggling for control of the pistol. Nadine coughed and sputtered, white powder covering her face and blouse. Beth joined Shannon, and together, they managed to knock the woman's arm against the wall. The gun fell out of her hand, but Nadine twisted and broke free from their grip. She ran, stumbling, and retreated down the steps.

Shannon picked up the gun and the two women chased after her. They caught up with her as she tried to navigate the dim passageway. Still trying to wipe the talc from her eyes, Nadine was no match for them. Beth restrained her while Shannon used the Hermes scarf Nadine wore to tie the woman's hands together behind her back.

Nadine began to scream. "Help me! Snake!"

"We've got to keep her from screaming," Shannon said, trying to stifle Nadine with her hand. "Och! She bit me."

Beth pulled off one shoe and removed her sock. "This should work."

Nadine saw what she intended and screamed even louder. "Don't you dare put that filthy thing near my mouth! Snaaaaaaaaaaake!"

Beth balled up the sock and stuck it in her screaming mouth. "What do we do now?"

"We call for help," Shannon said. "I have a cellphone in my room. Before I forget, what's the number for emergencies here?"

"It's 911."

The two-way radio clipped to Nadine's waist came to life. "Where are you, Miss?"

Nadine's eye widened. She began to squirm, trying to talk through the sock.

Beth bit her lip. "I'll take care of it."

She plucked the device off Nadine's waist, cleared her throat, and delivered a passable imitation of Nadine's voice. "On my way, pet."

"Stay here," Shannon said. "I'm going to get my phone." Shannon dashed off to her room, but to her dismay, she discovered her phone was dead. She hurried to rejoin her mother and found her standing in the hall near the landing of the main staircase, Nadine in her grasp.

"What are you doing?" Shannon whispered. "I told you to stay put."

"I thought we'd try and sneak out the front. Did you call the police?"

Shannon shook her head. "My phone's dead."

"Oh, no. What should we do?"

Shannon pulled the pistol out of her pocket. "I'm worried about Deborah. We can't leave her down there alone with that man. Who knows what he'll do?"

"No worries, girls." Snake's unmistakable accent rang out, echoing up the grand staircase.

He stood next to the bottom step, pointing a 9mm gun at them. Shannon gripped the pistol at her side.

"I know you think you're a clever lass, but I see that gun in your hand," he said. "Nice and slow, I want you to hold it in front of you by the barrel and come down the steps."

Shannon looked at Beth.

Her mother's voice caught as she spoke. "You'd better do as he says."

Shannon held the gun as instructed and descended the staircase.

"Good girl. Now hand it over." Shannon placed the gun

in Snake's outstretched hand, trying to ignore the other gun he still pointed at her head.

Beth and Nadine descended the stairs at a slower pace.

"You OK, Miss?" he asked Nadine as she approached. She nodded, groaning against the sock. "I knew something was wrong. I could feel it in my bones."

"Please, let us go," Shannon said. "There is no necklace. You can walk out of here, and we'll act like none of this ever happened."

Snake laughed. "Dream on, sweetheart. You and I still have a little score to settle." He pointed to Nadine. "Remove the sock from her mouth and untie her."

Beth did as he instructed.

With her chin held high, Nadine proceeded to spit powder out of her mouth and dust it off her clothing, wiping her face with the scarf that had bound her. Then she turned to Beth, raised her right arm, and struck her hard across the cheek.

Beth cried out as she brought a hand to her face.

"You will pay for what you've done here today," Nadine vowed. She looked from Beth to Shannon. "Both of you."

"Why do you hate us so much?" Shannon cried out, hoping to stall the inevitable.

"Because you're just like her. Everything came so easy to Victoria. Everything she touched turned to gold. Why did she get all the talent, all the luck, everything? Answer me that!"

"I'm sure that's not true. You've got—"

"Oh, shut up! I don't want to hear the phony praise of a sniveling brat. I just want you to be quiet."

She retrieved her pistol from Snake and batted at her hair with the other hand, releasing a cloud of scented powder into the air.

Snake waved his gun at the women. "Now march yourselves into the kitchen."

They followed Nadine into the kitchen, Snake trailing behind. Deborah's eyes widened when she saw them approach.

"Do you have enough for both of them?" Nadine asked.

Snake grinned and held up a large coil of rope.

"Tie them up. Then we'll figure out what to do with them."

"But I know where the necklace is!" Shannon blurted.

"Do you?" Nadine looked her over. "That's strange, considering you had no idea earlier."

"I figured it out right before you fired the gun."

Nadine's expression darkened. "You mean right before you attacked me like a wild animal."

"Right." Shannon swallowed. "There's a tile in the floor that's loose. I noticed it while looking through the cabinets. I believe the necklace is hidden underneath it."

Nadine noticed Beth edge away. "Don't just stand there, tie her up," she barked at Snake. Shannon watched as he set his gun down before reaching for the rope.

Nadine turned her full attention back to Shannon. "You have five minutes to retrieve it. If you aren't back in time, I'll shoot Deborah and your mother and disappear."

A sick feeling rose in Shannon's stomach. What if she was wrong? What if there was nothing under the tile? What if Nadine intended to shoot all three of them anyway?

I have to try.

"If I give you the necklace, no one gets hurt, right?" Shannon asked. "There's no need to shoot anyone. You can take it and leave."

Nadine raised her hand to her chin. "All right, you've got a deal."

"But you said I could keep the little feisty one," Snake whined, looking at Shannon.

She gasped, repulsion rippling through her.

"Hush. The clock's ticking, Shannon. You'd better get moving." Nadine threw back her head and cackled. "I'm actually having fun with this, aren't you, my pet?"

"I *was*," Snake pouted.

The echoes of her twisted humor followed Shannon as she bolted up the stairs. She ran through the darkened closet, tripping over hatboxes. Stumbling along, she finally made it to the turret, her adrenaline racing.

She knelt by the loosened tile and tried to wedge her fingernails in the tiny gap around it. They weren't long enough. She needed something long and skinny. *The hatpin.* Using the pin, she pried the tile up until she could grasp its edge. Then she grabbed it with both hands and thrust it aside. Underneath lay a black box similar to the one they'd found in the fireplace flue. But this one was much larger.

Lifting the lid confirmed her suspicion. A dazzling array of diamonds sparkled up at her in the glow of the red light. But there was no time to admire them.

She returned the hatpin to her sleeve, replaced the lid on the box, and hurried back the way she'd come.

"Ticktock, ticktock ..." She could hear Nadine mocking

her from the kitchen.

When she reached the bottom of the main staircase, she stopped dead in her tracks. Michael stood in the foyer, gun poised. She swallowed a scream as he held a finger to his lips.

Friend or foe? They made eye contact for a brief moment. *I have to trust him. I don't have a choice.*

"Distract," he mouthed.

She nodded and raced into the kitchen. "I'm back," she panted, bending over to catch her breath. "Don't shoot anybody."

Nadine checked her watch. "I'm impressed. Do you have it?"

Shannon held out the box.

"Sit down and remove the lid," Nadine commanded, gripping the pistol.

Shannon lowered herself to the cool tile and pulled off the lid. The sparkle of the diamonds lit up the old woman's eyes.

Nadine yanked the box out of Shannon's grasp with her free hand. "These are magnificent. My sister had exquisite taste."

With Nadine's attention focused entirely on the jewels, Shannon seized the opportunity. She slid the hatpin out of her sleeve and plunged it into the soft flesh behind Nadine's knee. Her great-aunt let out a piercing scream as she dropped the box and the pistol.

Shannon quickly reached for the gun.

"Freeze," Snake ordered. "Have you forgotten I have a gun too? I don't know what to think about you, lady. You're either pathetically stupid or incredibly brave."

"She's brave. Don't move." Michael appeared in the doorway, his gun drawn. "Put your gun down, slowly."

Shannon snatched the gun off the floor and scooted away from Nadine. She pointed the pistol at Snake from the other side of the room.

Snake hesitated just for a moment, then lowered his gun to the floor.

"You fool!" Nadine screamed. "I should've known someone who goes by the name 'Snake' wouldn't have a shred of intelligence in his head."

Sirens sounded and tires screeched in the drive. Chief Grayson and two officers burst through the front door. Shannon untied Deborah and Beth as Michael and the officers restrained Nadine and Snake.

"Shannon, darling," Nadine pleaded as handcuffs closed around her wrists. "This is all a big misunderstanding. I don't know how we came to this. Perhaps if we could sit down and have a cup of tea, we could resolve this in a civilized manner."

"Oh, I understand perfectly well," Shannon replied. "You want what's mine, and you'll do anything to get it—including armed robbery. Good luck working *that* out with the judge."

Nadine's lips curled into a sneer. "You think you're so clever. You'll soon find out there's more to this town than meets the eye—dark truths you'll wish you never knew." Officer Brownley tugged on the old woman's arm and dragged her away. That didn't stop her from shrieking a warning: "You will regret your decision to stay here, mark my words!"

"Don't listen to her," Beth said. "She's just a crazy old bat."

"I know." Shannon took a deep breath. Then she turned away and stepped out onto the patio to collect herself. A few minutes later, after the commotion inside settled, Michael joined her.

"Are you all right?" he asked before she had the chance to speak.

"I'm fine." She searched his face. "How did you know?"

"A client tipped me off. After I met with him, I did a little research and found out Nadine is up to her eyeballs in debt. I started following her and discovered she keeps very interesting company. She's been meeting with your former store manager and a clerk from the attorney's office on the sly. If I were a betting man, I'd put all my money on Nadine as the source of your brake failure and the threats you've received, both here and in Scotland."

"I'm so thankful you got here when you did," Shannon said. "And I owe you an apology for my horrible behavior the other day at the beach. I didn't even give you a chance to explain."

"No, I'm the one who's sorry. I should've been here sooner. When Victoria retained me for this job, I grossly underestimated the danger you'd be in." He raked a hand through his hair. "Nadine slipped away before I knew where she was headed or what she intended to do."

"Don't be sorry. Your timing was perfect." A smile flushed Shannon's face. Without thinking, she threw her arms around him and gave him a big hug. "I can't thank you enough, Michael. You saved us. Without your help, I'm afraid to imagine what might have happened."

He staggered back a step, caught off guard. He moved

to wrap his arms around her, but before he could do so, she released her hold on him and darted away. They stared at each other, an awkward silence between them.

After a moment, a slow smile began to spread across Michael's face. "I suppose now is as good a time as any to say it."

"Say what?"

"Welcome to Apple Grove. I'm glad you've decided to stay."

* * *

Later that night, Shannon lay in bed, unable to fall to sleep. Finding the necklace after all of the effort had been worth it. A stunning piece dripping with precious stones, its sale would provide enough for upkeep of the property and renovations to the craft market.

Then her thoughts returned to her mother. *What kind of relationship will we have? What do we do now?* She still had a million questions. And it was obvious those questions weren't going to allow her to sleep.

She slipped on her robe and descended the stairs in her bare feet. She intended to relax in the study, perhaps knit a few rows, until her eyes gave in to sleep. But as she approached, she noticed a line of light under the study door.

Alarmed, she cracked it open. Inside, Beth lay curled up on the loveseat.

"What are you doing in here?"

Beth's gaze surveyed the room, a nostalgic expression on her face. "Mother's study has always been special to me."

Shannon sat down beside her.

"Did you have trouble sleeping too?" Beth asked.

"Yes."

"When you were little and couldn't sleep, I would sing you a lullaby. You'd lay your head on my lap, and I'd sing and sing until you nodded off."

"How did it go?"

Beth closed her eyes and began to sing a sweet Scottish lullaby, a song Shannon remembered singing to her own children. She leaned over, and after a few tentative tries, rested her head on her mother's shoulder.

Turn the page for an exclusive preview of
the next mystery in the
Creative Woman Mysteries series.

A Deadly Stitch

COMING SOON!

— 1 —

The weather turned out perfect for Dedication Day—sunny, with bright blue skies and a cool, refreshing breeze.

Rows of chairs set up on the side lawn of the craft market began to fill up. Shannon took her place behind the podium, smiling at the small crowd. *What a glorious day for a celebration.* She'd hired a vocal group to sing and entertain, and several local vendors to serve up refreshments.

She tapped the microphone once to test it. The ping reverberated, proving it was hot. Gazing out at the audience, she saw many familiar faces. Her mother sat in a chair in the very front row, right next to her friends Betty, Joyce, Kate, and Melanie, all dolled up in their best outfits for the occasion. Essie also sat nearby. Chief Grayson, Harry, Deborah, and her sister, Gertrude, were all there. But there was one face in particular she didn't see.

Michael.

She cleared her throat and began: "As those of you who are familiar with me know, I come from a small coastal town in Scotland. It's a place with people who are proud of their traditions. People who are warm and friendly and love their families. They are a people much like the gracious and wonderful population of Apple Grove, my newly adopted town."

A smattering of applause sounded, then faded as she resumed her speech.

“It’s easy to see why my grandmother loved living here. Today, in the spirit of Victoria’s generous heart, I wish to continue her legacy of charitable contribution.”

The small crowd erupted into full-blown applause. She noticed the Purls clapped louder and longer than anyone else. Betty even put her thumb and index finger in her mouth and let out a whistle.

“To do so, we will sacrifice part of our stockroom and all of the garden landscaping in order to launch Espresso Yourself, a public coffeehouse and workroom space dedicated to craft groups who come together to create, display, and sell items to raise money for charitable organizations.”

She paused as she noticed a familiar stride. Michael approached the crowd and stood near the back. He smiled when she spotted him.

Shannon swallowed hard. “And now, without further ado, I’m going to attempt to break ground.”

As had been prearranged, Essie approached the podium bearing a yellow hard hat and a shovel. Shannon donned the hat, and chose a spot in the middle of the garden. Determined to dig out an impressive chunk rather than the ceremonial shovelful, she plunged the shiny new shovel deep into the soil, hoisted the dirt, and tossed it aside.

The crowd clapped again, and she signaled the man waiting with a backhoe to proceed.

She moved a few steps out of his way as he began to dig, and turned to face her friends with a triumphant smile on her face. Then the applause dwindled, and a few people in the front row stood up to point at something behind her.

Shannon turned to look as the backhoe ground to a

halt. A blue tarp stuck up from the dirt, wrapped around a large object.

Michael pushed through the crowd and stood next to her for a moment before crouching down closer for a better look.

Chief Grayson joined them. "What is it, Stone?"

"Judging by the smell ..." He pulled a handkerchief from his coat and held it to his nose, then pulled a section of the tarp away. "... it's a body."

Grayson looked over Stone's shoulder. He lifted his cap up from his forehead. "Oh boy." He pulled the radio off his duty belt and began to issue orders.

Shannon stared in disbelief. "Do you know who it is?"

A woman behind her began to scream. Shannon whirled to find Melanie standing there, staring at the body.

"No, no, no!" she screamed.

Joyce and Kate rushed to Melanie's side just as her face turned ghostly white and her legs gave out.

"I know who it is," Grayson muttered. "It's Edward, Melanie's ex-husband."